THE END

OF TRAGEDY

Four Novellas

RACHEL INGALLS

SIMON AND SCHUSTER

NEW YORK · LONDON · TORONTO · SYDNEY · TOKYO

Simon and Schuster
Simon & Schuster Building
Rockefeller Center
1230 Avenue of the Americas
New York, New York 10020

This book is a work of fiction. Names, characters, places and incidents are either the product of the author's imagination or are used fictitiously. Any resemblance to actual events or locales or persons, living or dead, is entirely coincidental.

Originally published in Great Britain by Faber & Faber Limited

SIMON AND SCHUSTER and colophon are registered trademarks
of Simon & Schuster Inc.

Designed by Eve Metz
Manufactured in the United States of America

1   3   5   7   9   10   8   6   4   2

Library of Congress Cataloging in Publication data

Ingalls, Rachel.
The end of tragedy / Rachel Ingalls.
p. cm.

Contents: Friends in the country—An artist's life—In the act
—The end of tragedy.
I. Title
PS3559.N38E54 1989   88-11549
813'.54—dc 19   CIP

ISBN 0-671-66037-3

CONTENTS

FRIENDS IN THE COUNTRY

It took them an hour to leave the house. Jim kept asking Lisa where things were and why she hadn't bought such and such; if she'd intended to buy that thing there, then she should have warned him beforehand. "Otherwise," he told her, "we duplicate everything and it's a waste of money. Look, now we've got two flashlights."

She let the shopping bag drop down on the floor with a crash. "Right. That's one for you and one for me," she said. "And then we won't have to argue about it when we split up."

His face went set in an expression she recognized. He'd skipped two intermediate phases and jumped to the stage where, instead of being hurt, he started to enjoy the battle and would go for more provocation, hoping that they'd begin to get personal. "In that case," he said, "I hosie the blue one."

She laughed. She leaned against the wall, laughing, until he had to join in. He said, "We can keep the black one in the car, I guess. It might come in useful."

"You think we should phone them?"

He shook his head. He didn't know anything about this Elaine—she was Nancy's friend—but he was pretty sure her cousin wouldn't want to begin eating before eight on a Friday night, especially not if she lived out of town. "And they shouldn't anyway," he added. "Eight-thirty would be the right time."

"But some people do. If you're working nine to five, and if you—"

"Then they ought to know better."

There were further delays as he wondered whether to take a bottle of wine, and then how good it had to be if he did. Lisa heard him rooting around in the kitchen as she stared closely into the bathroom mirror. She smeared a thin film of Vaseline

7

on the tips of her eyelashes, put her glasses on, took them off and leaned forward. Her nose touched the glass. Jim began to yell for her to hurry up. Her grandfather used to do the same thing; she could remember him shouting up the stairs for her grandmother; and then if there was still no result, he'd go out and sit in the car and honk the horn. Jim hadn't learned that extra step yet, but he might think of it at any minute. They'd been living together for only a few months. She was still a little worried that one day he might get into the car and drive off without her.

They were out of the house, in the car, and halfway down the street when she remembered that she'd left the bathroom light on. She didn't say anything about it. They moved on toward the intersection. Jim was feeling good, now that they'd started: the passable bottle of wine being shaken around in the backseat, the new flashlight in the glove compartment. He looked to the left and into the mirror.

She tried not to breathe. She always hated the moment of decision—when you had to hurl your car and yourself out into the unending torrent of the beltway. Jim loved it. They dashed into the stream.

The rush hour was already beginning, although the sky was still light. Pink clouds had begun to streak the fading blue of the air. When they got off the freeway and onto the turnpike, the streetlamps had been switched on. They drove down a country road flanked by frame houses.

"What did that map say?" he asked.

"Left by the church, right at the school playing field."

They were supposed to go through three small towns before they came to the driveway of the house but—backtracking from the map—they got lost somewhere around the second one and approached the place from behind. At any rate, that was what they thought.

They sat in the car with the light on and pored over the map. Outside it didn't seem to be much darker, because a fog had begun to mist over the landscape. He blamed her for misdirecting him, while she repeated that it wasn't her fault: not if he'd worked it out so carefully beforehand; she couldn't see all those itsy-bitsy names in the dark, and anyway she'd said for him to go exactly the way he'd instructed her.

"Well," he said, "this should do it. Can you remember left—right—left?"

"Sure," she answered. And so could he; that was just the kind of thing he'd told her back at the house.

He started the car again and turned out the light. They both said, "Oh," and "Look," at the same time. While they'd been going over the map, the fog had thickened to a soupy, gray-blue atmosphere that filled the sky and almost obscured the trees at the side of the road. Jim drove slowly. When the road branched, he said, "Which way?"

"Left—right—left."

They passed three other cars, all coming from the opposite direction. As the third one went by them, he said, "At least it doesn't lead to nowhere."

"Unless it's to somewhere else."

"Meaning what?"

"I don't know," she said. "It just came to me."

"Wonderful. You should be working for the government. Which way now?"

"To the right."

"And there's a street sign up ahead. At last."

When they got near enough to the sign to make out what it said, they saw that it didn't have any writing on it at all. It was white, with a red triangle painted on it, and inside the triangle was a large, black shape.

"That's great," she said. "What's it supposed to mean— black hole ahead?"

"Look, there's another one. The whole damn road's full of them. What's the black thing? Come on, you can see that."

Lisa opened her window. The signs were as closely spaced as trees or ornamental bushes planted along a street to enhance its beauty and give shade during the summer.

She leaned her head out and looked at the black object inside the red triangle.

"It's like a kind of frog," she said, pulled her head back in and shut the window. She'd just realized that she hadn't brought her glasses with her; not that it really mattered for a

single dinner party, but she always liked to have them with
her in case she had to change her eye makeup under a bad
light, or something like that.

"I remember now," he told her. "Its OK. I've just never
seen it before. It's one of those special signs for the country."

"What?"

"They signpost all the roads they've got to cross to get to
their breeding grounds or spawning places, or something.
People run over so many of them when it's the season.
They're dying out."

"Frogs?"

"No, not frogs. Toads."

"I hope it isn't their breeding season now. That's all we
need."

"Which way at the crossroads?"

"Left."

In fifteen minutes they came to a white-painted wooden
arrow set low in the ground. It said "Harper" and led them
onto a narrow track. The headlights threw up shadowy
patterns of tree branches. Leaves brushed and slapped
against the sides of the car.

"This better be it," he said.

"Otherwise we break open the wine and get plastered."

They lurched along the last curve of the drive and out into
a wide, graveled space, beyond which stood a building that
looked like a medievalized Victorian castle. Lisa giggled. She
said, "So this is where your friends live."

Jim reached into the backseat for the wine and said he
hoped so, because otherwise it was going to be a long ride to
anywhere else.

The door was opened by someone they couldn't see. Jim
stepped forward into darkness and tripped. Lisa rushed after
him. There was a long creak and the heavy door groaned,
then slammed behind them.

"Are you all right?" she asked. She fell on top of him.

"Look out," he said. "The wine." It took a while for
them to untangle themselves. They rose to their feet like

survivors of a shipwreck who suddenly find themselves in the shallows.

They could see. They could see that the hallway they stood in was weakly lit by a few candles, burning high up on two separate stands that resembled iron hat racks; each one expanded into a trident formation at the top. The candles were spitted on the points.

Lisa turned to Jim, and saw that a man was standing in back of him. She gave a squeak of surprise, nearly blundering against a second man, who was stationed behind her. Both men were tall, dressed in some kind of formal evening wear that included tails; the rest of the outfit looked as if it might have been found in an ancient theatrical wardrobe trunk. "Your coat, sir," the one next to Jim said. He held out his arms.

By the time their coats had been removed and the bottle plucked from Jim's hands, they were ready for anything.

One of the men led them down a corridor. Like the hallway, it was dark. The floor sounded as if it might be tile. The air was cold and smelled unpleasant. Lisa reached for Jim's hand.

The tall man in the lead threw open a double door. Light came rushing out in a flow of brilliance. In front of them lay a bright, inviting room: glass-topped tables, gilded mirrors, chrome and leather armchairs in black and white, semicircular couches. There were eight other people in the room. They'd been laughing when the door had opened on them. Now they were turned toward Jim and Lisa as if the room had become a stage set and they were the cast of a play.

"Your guests, madam," the first butler said. He snapped the doors shut behind him.

A woman who had been standing by the mantelpiece came forward. She had on a long, blackish velvet gown and what at first appeared to be a headdress, but which—seen closer—was actually her own dark hair piled up high; lines of pearls were strung out and perched in wavy configurations along the ridges and peaks of the structure.

Jim let go of Lisa's hand. She could feel how embarrassed he was. He'd be fighting the urge to jam his hands into his pockets.

"Um," he began, "Elaine—"

"We thought you'd never get here," the woman said. "I'm Isabelle."

She took his hand lightly in hers and let it go again almost immediately. Then she repeated the action as Jim made the introductions. Lisa realized that although the woman was certainly middle-aged and not particularly slim, she was beautiful. But something was wrong with the impression she gave. She had enough natural magnificence to carry her opera diva getup without appearing ridiculous; and yet she seemed out of date. And the touch of her hand had been odd.

Isabelle introduced them around the room. Dora and Steve, the couple nearest to them, were gray-haired. Steve wore a gray flannel suit that might once have been office regulation but at the moment looked fairly shapeless. Dora sported a baggy tweed jacket and skirt. Both husband and wife were pudgily plump, and they wore glasses: his, an old-fashioned pair of horn-rims; hers, an extraordinary batwing design in neon blue, with rhinestones scintillating at the tips. It came out in subsequent conversation that the two were school-teachers and that they were interested in the occult.

Isabelle gave no hint as to the marital status of the next four people introduced: who was paired with whom, and in what way. There were two women and two men. The women were both young: Carrol, a plain girl with long, straight orange hair and a knobbly, pale face; Jeanette, pretty and brunette, who had shiny brown eyes and a good figure. She was an airline stewardess.

"And Dr. Benjamin," Isabelle said.

The doctor bowed and said, "Oh, how do you do." He was a small, stooped man, just beginning to go white at the temples. He reminded Lisa a little of the father of a girl she'd been to school with.

"And Neill. You probably recognize him." The young man Isabelle indicated gave Jim and Lisa each an effortless, charming smile, just specially for them. He said, "A lot of people don't watch TV."

"I'm afraid we don't," Jim said. "We get home tired, and then we eat." And then they jumped into bed, or else they did that before eating, or sometimes before and after too, but they hadn't watched much television for months.

"Are you in plays and things?" Lisa asked.

"I'm in a megasoap called *Beyond Love*. The cast calls it *Beyond Hope*, or sometimes *Beyond Belief*. It really is."

"What's it about?"

"The short version, or the twenty-three-episode breakdown?"

"We all adore it," Isabelle said. "We miss it dreadfully now that the electricity's going haywire again. We were hoping to watch it over the weekend."

"Just as well you can't," Neill said.

"Not another shooting? They aren't writing you out of the script, are they?"

"I think this is the one where I lose an arm. My illegitimate father whips me from the house, not knowing that—you did say the short version, didn't you?"

Isabelle said she didn't believe any of it and he'd better behave. "And finally," she told Lisa and Jim, as she swayed ahead of them over the satiny rug, "my husband, Broderick." She left her hand open, her arm leading them to look at the man: swarthy, barrel-chested, bald and smiling. He looked like a man of power, an executive of some kind, who relaxed while others did the work he'd set up for them. He was leaning against the mantelpiece. The introductions had brought Jim and Lisa full circle in the room.

"A quick drink," Isabelle suggested, pouncing gracefully upon two full glasses next to a silver tray. She handed them over, saying, "Our very own mixture, guaranteed harmless, but it does have some alcohol in it. If you'd rather have fruit juice—"

Lisa was already sipping at her drink. The glass was like an oversized martini glass but the cocktail wasn't strong, or didn't seem to be. It tasted rather delicate; herblike, yet pleasant. "This is fine," she said.

"Sure," Jim added. She knew he wouldn't like it but would be agreeing in order to be polite.

"Now, we're going to move to the dining room soon, so if any of you ladies need a sweater or a shawl, there's a pile over there. Or bring your own from your rooms." She said to Jim, "It's such a nuisance—we have to keep most of the rooms a little underheated. Something to do with the boiler."

"Not the boiler," Broderick said.

"Well, pipes, or whatever it is. Poor Broderick—he's suffered miseries over it."

"On the contrary. I just kicked out those two jokers who were trying to fleece us for their so-called work, and that's why we're up the creek now. Can't get anybody else for another three weeks. Maybe it'll get better tomorrow. It ought to be a lot warmer at this time of year."

"It wasn't bad in town," Jim said. "I guess you must be in a kind of hollow. We hit a lot of fog. That's why we were late."

"Yes, it's notorious around here," Isabelle said. "The locals call it Foggy Valley."

One of the mournful butlers opened the double doors again and announced that dinner was served. Jim and Lisa tilted their glasses back. On the way out with the others, Lisa lifted a shawl from a chair near the doorway. All the other women had picked up something before her.

Carrol sat on Jim's right, Jeanette at the left. He preferred Jeanette, who was cheerful, healthy-looking and pretty, but somehow he was drawn into talk with Carrol.

The room was intensely, clammily, cold. He started to drink a lot of wine in order to warm himself up. Lisa, across from him, was drinking too—much more than usual.

Carrol kept passing one of her pale, bony hands over her face, as if trying to push away cobwebs. She said that she'd felt very restless and nervous ever since giving up smoking. "I tried walking," she said. "They tell you to do that, but then I'd get back into the house and I'd want to start eating or smoking. So, I knit. But you can't take it everywhere. It sort of breaks up the conversation. And I'm not very good at it, even after all this time. I have to concentrate on the counting." She blinked several times, as if about to cry.

From his other side Jeanette said, "I guess we're all looking for different things. Except—I bet really they're not so different in the long run. In my case it was the planes. I'd get on and begin the routine, get everything working right, count the meals, look at the chart, see the passengers going in, and suddenly I'd just know: this one is going to crash."

"What did you do?" Jim asked.

"I got off. They were very nice about it when I explained. They didn't fire me. But they said I had to take therapy."

"And?"

"And I did. It was fine. It was a six-week course and it really made me feel a lot better. So, I went back to work again and everything was OK for another year. I thought I had it licked. And then it started up again, just like before. That's where I am now."

"What are you doing for it this time?"

"I'm here," Jeanette said.

Jim took another sip of the thick, brownish-red wine. It tasted dusty and bitter, although it seemed to be fairly potent, too. The bouquet reminded him of some plant or flower he couldn't place. He took another swallow. His feet were beginning to feel cold. "You mean, here to relax?" he said.

"I'm here to consult Isabelle and Broderick."

"Oh. And is that helping?"

"Of course. They're wonderful."

"They've helped me too," Carrol said. "No end."

The two cadaverous butlers managed the refilling of the wineglasses and the serving of the meal, the main course of which was a stew that they ladled out of an enormous green casserole.

Lisa looked longingly at the food as it started to be passed around. She wished that she'd taken two shawls with her instead of one. It wasn't just the cold, either, or the general darkness of the room; there was a distinctly disagreeable, dank smell emanating from the corners, from the floor under the lovely old rug. Perhaps there was some reason, connected with the low temperature, for the odor: mold, or that kind of thing. She'd suspected at first that it might be coming from the wine, which she'd nearly choked on; it was like taking a mouthful of plasma. Neill had asked for, and been given, two more cocktails. She was thinking that she should have done that herself, when he handed both glasses straight to her without asking if she wanted them.

She'd been seated between him and Dr. Benjamin. She turned her attention to the doctor first. "Are you a medical doctor?" she asked.

He said no and told her what he was, which she didn't understand. "Algae," he explained. "Pond life, biology." Then he made an encompassing gesture with his right hand and arm, adding, "But it's all connected, you know. The animal kingdom, the vegetable kingdom, fish, flowers, rocks, trees. Fascinating. We're only part of it."

"Oh," she said with delight, "yes." She'd caught his enthusiasm and all of a sudden she was drunk. She said to Neill, "I think I got a better deal on the cocktails. It's just hit me. What's in them?"

"I should have warned you—they're pretty strong. The ingredients are a closely guarded secret, but the rumor is that they're dill, parsley and vodka, with a squeeze of lemon and a touch of aniseed. But mostly vodka."

"Nice. Better than the wine."

"The wine is an acquired taste. You'll get to love it."

One of the butlers put a heaped plate of the stew in front of her. A rich, spicy aroma steamed up into her face. She looked toward Isabelle, who had lifted her fork, and dug in.

The food was nearly as strange as the wine. The meat had a tang like game. "What is it?" she asked, after she'd chewed the first mouthful.

"Chicken livers, I think," the doctor said. "Delicious."

Lis continued to eat. Surely they didn't make chickens that big. And anyway, the pieces of meat were so chewy and tough, you could almost imagine that they were parts of a bat.

"I've never tasted any chicken livers like this," she said.

"Oh, it's all health food," Dr. Benjamin assured her. "The flavors are much stronger and more natural. Our jaded palates aren't used to them."

"Except the wine," Neill said. "It isn't one of those health wines."

"Quite superb," the doctor agreed, raising his glass. The two men smiled at each other across Lisa. She bit down on another piece of her meat and hit a horny substance that resisted. It was too slippery to get back onto her fork again. She chewed rapidly, then gave up, reached in, quickly took it out of her mouth and put it on the side of her plate. It was a large, rubbery black triangle of cartilage. Her glance darted to the side. The doctor had noticed.

"Wonderful stuff," he pronounced. "Terrific for the spleen."

"If you can get it that far," she said.

"It's good for the teeth and gums to have to chew."

"That's true," Neill said. "I've got caps. Anything happens to them, it's my salary in danger. But I've never hit a bone in this house. You can relax." He began to talk about the degree to which a television actor was dependent on his face, how you began to look at yourself completely dispassionately, as if seeing a mask from the outside. And then you stuck the emotions on afterward. To do it the other way—beginning with the emotion and building toward the outward expression—was so exhausting that you could kill yourself like that, or go crazy. "You can go crazy in any case. I started to flip about three years ago. That's why I'm here."

"I thought actors were supposed to like pretending and showing off."

"It was the series. Autosuggestion. I got to the point where I'd think the things they were making up in the story were actually happening to me. Those characters in the soaps— they really go through it, you know. It was like living that crap. It broke up my life. Broke up my marriage."

"You got divorced?" she asked. "Separated?"

"It started with a coldness. Then there was an estrange-ment."

He stopped speaking. The mention of cold had made her conscious once more of the chilling damp. It seemed to be pulling the room down into ever darker and deeper layers of rawness.

"Then," he said, "she took the children and left, and got the divorce."

"That's awful," Lisa said. She looked at him with sympathy, but he smiled back, saying, "It turned out to be all for the best. It's how I found this place. I'd never have known how far gone I was. I wouldn't have tried to get help. Maybe an analyst, maybe not. But now I'm fine."

"How?"

"Broderick and Isabelle."

"Are they doctors?"

"He's a healer. She's a medium. They don't advertise it or anything. They aren't in it for the money, like the fakes."

Just for the power, Lisa thought. She was surprised that a couple who looked as capable as Broderick and Isabelle should be mixed up in the occult. That, she thought, was for people like Dora and Steve.

"I take it you're not a believer," he said.

"Oh, I believe in faith healing. That's half of medicine. Well, not half. Forty-five percent."

"You'll come to see the rest, too," Dr. Benjamin told her complacently. She felt angry suddenly. She didn't know what she was doing at this stupid dinner, with these weird people, in a freezing room and eating such revolting food. Even the liquor was peculiar. She tried to catch Jim's eye, but he was stuck with Carrol.

The dessert arrived: a minty sherbet that hadn't set right. The constituents were already separating, and the areas not beginning to melt were oozing and slimy. Lisa took one bite and left the rest. The aftertaste was peppery. Jim finally looked at her from across the table. He gave her a defeated smile. She almost made a face back.

"Coffee in the living room?" Isabelle asked the table. She stood up. Everyone followed. Lisa went straight to Jim. She whispered that she hoped they'd be cutting the evening short, right after the coffee. He nodded and whispered back, "You bet."

"They're some kind of psychic health freaks," she said.

"They cure people of psychosomatic things. Fears and stuff."

"I've got a fear of horrible food."

"Jesus, yes. Even the rolls and butter."

"I didn't see them."

"It was sort of like trying to eat my jacket."

They wanted to stay together but Broderick moved them to chairs where they'd be near the people they hadn't sat with at dinner. Lisa was expected to talk to Dora; the heat of the room felt so good that she didn't mind. She attempted to look interested, while Dora spoke about the difficulty of finding a really good nursery. For several minutes Lisa thought they were talking about children.

She was handed a cup of coffee and lifted it to her lips. It was black, scalding, acrid, and didn't taste like coffee. It was like trying to drink a cup of boiling urine. She set it back on its saucer and looked across the room. Isabelle's neat hands were still busied with the silver pot and the cups. Carrol was actually drinking the stuff; so were Neill and Jeanette and Dr. Benjamin. Dora's husband, Steve, was positively slurping his with enjoyment.

She watched Jim take his first swallow. His nostrils flared, his eyes screwed tight for a moment.

"And that's the most important thing, isn't it?" Dora said.

"What?"

"The soil."

"Of course. Basic," Lisa said. She knew nothing about gardening. When her sister had been out in the backyard helping their mother to do the weeding, she'd stayed indoors to draw and cut up pieces of colored paper. She said, "Do you teach botany at your school?"'

"Biology."

"Like the doctor."

"He's a specialist. Most of his work is done through the microscope."

"I guess a lot of his job must be finding out how to get rid of all the chemical pollution around."

"It's a crime," Dora said. "Is that your field?"

"I work for a museum," Lisa told her. "I help to plan the exhibition catalogs and everything."

"How interesting."

It wasn't actually very interesting so far, because she was right at the bottom, just picking up after the other people who did the real work. But someday it was going to be fine: she'd travel, and do her own designs, and be in charge. The only trouble would be trying to fit everything in so that it worked out with Jim.

She could see that Dora was about to go back to biology when Jim stood up at the far end of the room. Lisa said, "Excuse me just a minute." She got up and joined him.

He was talking to Isabelle, who had made him sit down again, beside her on the couch; she was saying, "But you can't." She looked up at Lisa. "You can't possibly just run off. You're staying for the weekend."

Lisa sat next to Jim. She said, "Just for dinner, I thought?" She took him by the arm and dug her fingers in.

"It's very nice of you," he said, "but we must have gotten the signals wrong. We don't even have a toothbrush between us."

"Oh, we can lend you everything."

"And Aunt Alice tomorrow," Lisa said, "and Mrs. Havelock at church on Sunday." She'd used the same made-up names for the past year; ever since the evening when she'd flung a string of them at Jim and he'd repeated them, getting every one wrong. Now they had a private pantheon: Aunt Alice, Mrs. Havelock, Cousin George, the builders, the plumber, the twins, Grandmother and Uncle Bob, Norma and Freddie, and the Atkinsons.

"I'm afraid it's too late in any case," Isabelle said. "The fog here gets very bad at night around this time of the year. I don't think you'd be able to see your hand in front of your face."

"It's true," Jeanette said. "I took a look before we sat down. It's really socked in out there."

"If it's anything urgent," Isabelle suggested, "why don't you phone, and stay over, and then you can leave in the morning. All right? We'd rather have you stay on, though. And we were counting on the numbers for tomorrow night."

Jim turned to look at Lisa. If the fog was worse than when they'd arrived, there was probably nothing they could do. He said, "I guess—"

"If we start off early in the morning," Lisa said. "It's nice of you to ask us."

"I'll show you the way right now," Isabelle told them.

Lisa stared at the huge bed. It was the biggest one she'd ever seen and it was covered in a spread that looked like a tapestry. The room too was large; it seemed about the size of a double basketball court. Everything in it was gloomy. All the colors were dark and muddy. The main lighting came from above: a tiny triple-bulbed lamp pronged into the ceiling above the bed and worked from a switch by the door. There was also a little lamp on a table at the far side of the room.

"This old place," Isabelle said. "I'm afraid the bathrooms are down the hall. Do bear with us. We try to make up in hospitality. Broderick simply loves it here—his family's been in the district just forever. But I must say, I can never wait for the holidays. Then we go abroad to Italy. When the children come back from school."

"How many children do you have?" Lisa asked.

"Three boys. I don't know why I keep calling them children. They're already taller than their father—hulking great brutes."

Isabelle led them down the corridor to a bathroom that was nearly as big as the bedroom. There was a giant tub on claw feet, a toilet with a chain, and a shower partly hidden by a stained plastic curtain. The place was tiled halfway up to the high ceiling. In the corner opposite the toilet the tiles were breaking apart or disintegrating as if the cement had begun to crumble away.

Isabelle said, "I'll just go see about getting you some towels. We'll meet downstairs. All right?" She left them standing side by side in front of the bathrub.

Lisa whispered, "Some friends you've got."

"It's pretty weird."

"It's unbelievable. What was that stuff we were eating?"

"Jesus, I don't know. I kept trying to guess. I got something on my fork I thought was an ear, and then a hard piece that looked like part of a kneecap. It all tasted like . . . I don't know what."

"They're crazy, aren't they?"

"I doubt it. Pretentious, maybe. Dora and Steve are the crazy types: dull and normal on the surface, but really looking for leaders to show them their occult destiny."

"She's got a thing about soil. God, I wish we didn't have to stay over."

"At least it's warm up here," he said. "And they're right—it's like pea soup outside."

"First thing in the morning, we leave. Right?"

"Definitely. I get the strangest feeling when I'm talking to Broderick, you know. And Isabelle, too."

"I know what you mean."

"I mean really. As if there's something wrong. As if they're the wrong people, or there's been a mistake."

"I've just thought of something. Wouldn't it be funny if you didn't know them at all?"

"Well, I don't. They're friends of Elaine's parents. Or of her mother's cousin. Something like that."

"I mean, maybe we took the wrong road. Are you sure they're the right people? That sign we passed: the one that had a name on it—that isn't their name, is it? Or the name of Elaine's friends, either."

"Well . . . I don't know what we could do about it now, anyway."

"It really would be funny, wouldn't it?"

"And embarrassing. It would be just about the most embarrassing thing I can imagine."

"Oh, not that bad. Not after that fabulous meal they just gave us. And the coffee; how do you suppose they cooked that up?"

"Maybe they had those two butlers out in the pantry just spitting into a trough for a couple of days."

Lisa pulled the shower curtain to one side. "Look at this," she said, holding it wide to inspect the stains, which were brown and might almost have been taken for bloodstains. "The whole house." She pulled it farther. As she drew it away, she could see the corner of the shower. A mass of dead brown leaves lay heaped on the tiles. "See that?" she asked.

"Smells bad, too," Jim said.

They both stared down. Lisa leaned forward. Suddenly the leaves began to move, the clump started to split into segments.

Her voice was driven, growling, deep into her throat. She clapped her hands to her head and danced backward over the floor, hitting the opposite wall. Then she was out of the door and down the hallway. Jim dashed after her. He'd just caught up with her when they bumped into Isabelle.

Isabelle said, "Good heavens. What's happened?"

"Toads," Lisa groaned. "A whole gang of them. Hundreds."

"Oh dear, not again."

"Again?"

"At this time of year. But there's nothing to worry about. They're harmless."

"They carry viruses," Lisa babbled. "Subcutaneous viruses that cause warts and cancers."

"Old wives' tales," Isabelle laughed. "You just sit down and relax, and I'll deal with it." She continued along the corridor and down the stairs.

Jim put his arm around Lisa. She was shivering. She said, "I can't stay here. Jesus. Right in the house. Thousands of them. Please, Jim, let's just get into the car and go. If we're fogged in, we can stop and go to sleep in the backseat."

"We can't now," he said.

"Please. I'm grossing out."

"Just one night," he told her. "I'll be with you. It isn't as if they're in the bed."

"Oh, God. Don't." She started to cry. He hugged and kissed her. He felt bad for not having been able to resist the temptation to frighten her. It was so much fun to get the reaction.

"Come on," he said. "I'll try to find you a drink."

"Oh boy," she sniffed. "Some more of that wonderful coffee."

"They've got to have a real bottle of something, some-

where. If everything else fails, I'll ask for the one we brought
with us."

He led her back to the brightly lit living room. Broderick
stepped forward with a glass in his hand. "Say you forgive
us, please," he begged. "And take just one sip of this."

Lisa accepted the glass. She raised it to her lips. She wanted
to get out of the house and go home, and never remember the
place again. She let a very small amount of the liquid slide
into her mouth. It was delicious. She took a big gulp.

"Nice?" Broderick said.

"Terrific."

"Great. We'll get you another." He pulled her over to the
couch where Neill was sitting. Neill began to talk about
making a TV film in Italy one summer a few years ago:
Broderick and Isabelle had been there at the time. And
Broderick talked about a statisticians' conference he'd been
attending.

Everyone began to drink a great deal. Lisa felt wonderful.
She heard Jim and Carrol and Jeanette laughing together
across the room and saw Dora and Steve sitting on either side
of Isabelle, the doctor standing behind them. She had another
one of the drinks, which Broderick told her were coffee
liqueur plus several other things. She laughed with pleasure
as she drank. She wanted to hear more about Italy and the
museums and churches she'd only ever seen pictured in
books. It would be so nice, she said, to go there and see the
real thing in the real country.

But why didn't she? Broderick thought she certainly
should: go to Italy as soon as possible; come with them that
summer and stay at the villa. "Oh, wouldn't that be nice,"
she told him; "wouldn't it be just like a dream? But Jim's job.
And mine, too. . . ."

There was a break. She came back, as if out of a cloud, to
find herself in a different, smaller room, and lying on a couch
with Neill. She knew she was pretty drunk and she had no
idea if they'd made love or not. She didn't think so. They
both still had all their clothes on. Her head was heavy and
hurting.

As she moved, he kissed her. She sat up. He reached

toward her. She could see under his shirt a red patch composed of flaking sores. It looked as though the skin had been eaten away. "What's wrong with your chest?" she said.

"Makeup allergy. Badge of the trade. Come on back."

"I think I'd better be going. I'm pretty plastered."

"So's everybody."

"But I'd better go." She got up. He let her find her way out alone. She stumbled through hallways in near darkness, thinking that any minute she'd fall over or be sick. She came to the staircase and pulled herself up, leaning on the rail.

The bedroom was empty and autumnally moist. There was a smell, all around, of rotting leaves. A pair of pajamas and a nightgown had been draped over the foot of the bed. The sheet was turned down. She got undressed and climbed in.

The light was still on. She was thinking about having to get up again to turn it out, when Jim lumbered in. He threw himself on top of the bed, saying, "Christ, what a night. Where did you get to? I looked everywhere."

"I don't know," she said. "I feel terrible." She closed her eyes. When she opened them again, he was already sleeping. The light was still on. She turned her head and fell asleep herself.

When she woke again, the room was in darkness and stiflingly hot. The odor in the air had changed to one of burning. "Jim?" she said. She started to throw the covers back. He wasn't anywhere near. She felt around in the dark. It was so pitch-black that it was like being trapped in a hole under the ground. What she needed was a flashlight; they'd brought one with them—the black one—but it was still in the car. "Jim?" she said again. She sat up and clasped her knees. She was about to peel off the borrowed nightgown she was wearing, when he touched her hands.

"I can't sleep," she said. "It's so hot."

His hands moved from her finger down to her shins, to the hem of the nightdress and underneath it, up the inside of her legs, and rested on her thighs. She held his arms above the elbows. He sighed.

She said, "Let me get out of this thing," and was reaching down and back for the nightgown hem when a second pair of hands slid gently up the nape of her neck, and a third pair came forward and down over her breasts. Close to her right ear a fourth person laughed. She yelped. Her arms jerked up convulsively.

They were all on top of her at once. She whirled and writhed in the sheets and yelled as hard as she could for Jim, but they had their hands everywhere on her and suddenly she was lifted, thrown down again, and one of them—or maybe more than one—sat on her head. She couldn't do anything then; the first one had never let go of her legs.

She couldn't breathe. Two of them began to laugh again. She heard the nightdress being ripped up, and then, from a distance, the doorknob turning. Shapes bounded away from her across the bed. Light was in her eyes from the hall. And Jim was standing in the doorway. He switched on the ceiling lights.

She fell out of the bed, onto the rug, where she knelt, shuddering and holding her sides. She whined about the men: how many of them there were and what they'd been trying to do to her. The words weren't coming out right.

"What's wrong?" Jim demanded. He put down a glass he'd been carrying.

"Where were you?" she croaked.

"I went to get some water. What's wrong?"

"Men in here—four, six maybe, a whole crowd of them."

"When?"

"Just before you came in."

"They left before that?"

"The light scared them."

"Are you OK?"

"I guess so," she said.

He made her drink half the glass he'd brought back. "Which way did they go?" he asked.

"They're still here. Unless they ran past you when you opened the door."

"No," he said. He looked around. "There isn't anyone," he told her. "Look. Nobody here. Just us."

"They're under the bed."

"Come on."

"Take a look," she ordered. Her teeth started to chatter. She wrapped herself in the torn pieces of the nightgown.

He got down on his knees and peered sideways under the bed. "Nothing," he said.

She joined him and took a long look herself.

"See? Nobody," he said. "Nothing. Not very clean, but no other people."

"They were here."

"Look at your nightgown," he told her. "How much did you have to drink, anyway?"

"Not enough for all that."

"We could both use some sleep."

"I'm not staying in this room unless the light's on. I mean it. If you want the light out, I'm sleeping in the hall: I'm running out of the house. I won't stay here."

"Take it easy. You want the light on, we'll keep it on."

"And the door locked."

"I thought they were still in here."

"The door," she shouted.

He went to the door, which had a keyhole but no key. He pretended to be twisting something near the right place, and returned to the bed. He got in under the covers and put his arms around her.

"I can't wait to get home," she said. "Tomorrow. As early as possible."

"Um. But we might stay just a little."

"No."

"Broderick was telling me about this business deal he's got lined up. It sounds really good. We could travel, everything."

"Jim, we don't even know them. And this whole house is completely crazy. And all this occult crap, and—Jesus, nearly getting raped the minute you walk down the hall."

"I think we all had a lot to drink."

"Not that much."

"I didn't mean you. If there was anybody, maybe they thought this was the wrong room. Maybe it's part of that occult stuff they were talking about at dinner."

"Oh?"

"That would explain it, wouldn't it?"

"If you call that an explanation."

"There are even people who spend every weekend that way."

"Sure."

"They do."

"Not in this part of the world."

Broderick sat at the head of the breakfast table. He'd finished eating, but drank coffee as he read the papers. He was still in his pajamas and dressing gown. At the other end of the table Isabelle poured tea. She wore a floor-length housecoat that had a stand-up collar. Her hair was pulled high in a coiled knot.

They were in a different room from the one in which the last night's dinner had been laid. The windows looked directly onto a garden, although nothing was discernible of it other than the shadow of a branch next to the panes. Everything else was white with fog.

"Tea or coffee," Isabelle said, "or anything you like. Just tell Baldwin or Ronald if you don't see what you want on the sideboard."

The other young members of the party weren't yet down. Dr. Benjamin was seated on Isabelle's left. He dipped pieces of bread into an eggcup. Dora and Steve sat side by side; he was eating off her plate, she was buttering a piece of toast. "I just love marmalade," she said.

"Is it always like this?" Lisa asked, looking toward the windows.

"It's a little worse than usual today," Broderick said, "but it should break up by lunchtime. We'll just have to keep you occupied till then. Do you swim? We've got a marvelous swimming pool. Really. Art Nouveau tiles all over. This place used to belong to—who was it? A real dinosaur. But the pool is great. And it's got three different temperatures."

"I don't have a bathing suit," Lisa said.

"We've got lots of extra suits."

Lisa and Jim each ate an enormous breakfast. She looked at him swiftly as they rushed to the sideboard for third helpings.

They almost started to laugh. The food was entirely normal, and the coffee too.

The morning passed pleasantly. Broderick showed them over most of the house. Some of the rooms were light and modern, others old-looking and apparently moldering. "We used to rent parts of it out," he told them. "For a long time that whole side over there was used as a retreat by a religious organization that Isbelle's Aunt Theda was involved with. If we sold it, I guess somebody'd turn the place into a school. They all want me to sell. But I couldn't bear it. My parents bought this house when I was seven. I remember moving in."

There were a billiards room, a game room with Ping-Pong tables in it, a library. The pool was indeed magnificent. Jim and Lisa put on the suits they were offered. Broderick and Jeanette joined them. Neill sat in a canvas chair where it was dry; he said the chlorine made his skin allergy itch. And Carrol, who had sat down next to him, pulled out her knitting and shook her head. She was waiting, she said, for her consultation with Broderick.

Broderick swam for about ten minutes, got out of the pool and went up to Carrol. "Right," he said. She packed up the knitting without a word and left with him. Neill challenged the rest of them to a Ping-Pong match.

It was surprising, Lisa thought, how much she was enjoying herself. But after the Ping-Pong they passed through a hallway that had a window, and she rushed forward to look out. The world was still white, but it was as bright as electric light. The sun was going to burn off the fog quickly.

"We can start soon," she said to Jim.

"Well, not right away. We could stay for lunch."

"As soon as possible."

"It wouldn't be very polite."

"What happened last night wasn't very polite, either."

"Let's not start on that again."

"OK. Let's just get out fast."

"This thing Broderick talked abut—it sounds really good. It could make a big difference to us."

"Jim, for God's sake," she said.

"Just cool it, Lisa. There's no hurry." He pushed forward ahead of her and turned to the right. She leaned back against a green stone statue that held a bowl meant for flowers. She wondered if she had the strength of will to get into the car herself and just drive away on her own.

He had the keys. It was his car. And he was the invited guest, even if this wasn't the right house. All the embarrassment would be his to deal with after she'd gone. She couldn't really do that to him.

Jeanette met her at a turn in the corridor. "Are you staying for the season?" she asked.

"I don't think so. We'll be leaving pretty soon. We've got to get back to town."

"That's too bad. The sessions really help."

"In what way?"

"Well . . . just talking. Broderick says that fear—fear itself is a disease. Do you believe that?"

"To a certain extent. Sure."

"It helps to talk about it."

"It helps if the thing you're afraid of goes away. If you can make that happen by talking, I guess that's good."

"Of course you can. Because it's in the mind."

"The things I'm afraid of," Lisa said, "are definitely not in my mind. They're in the world."

"But if they haven't happened yet—"

"A little anticipation keeps us all alive. Right?"

"It keeps us frightened."

"Frightened people are careful. And careful people live longer."

"Sometimes it isn't worth it," Jeanette said.

They reached the breakfast room. Steve and Dora were still at the table. Sunlight streamed in through the windows.

She ran upstairs, got her purse and raced down again. She felt wonderful: the sun was out and at last they could leave.

Broderick met her at the foot of the stairs. "Where to, and so fast?" he said. He smiled jovially but his eyes gloated at her.

"We've really got to get back now," she said.

"But Jim said you were staying through lunch."

"I'm afraid not."

"It's all fixed. He said he'd phone whoever it was you had to meet."

"It isn't that simple. Where is he?"

"Out in the garden somewhere, I think. Want me to help you look?'"

"No, thanks," she said. "It's all right."

She stepped out the side door onto a brick terrace. Stairs led down to a garden of white-flowering bushes. Beyond them stood a statue of a woman, one signaling arm raised out of her marble drapery. Neill was sitting on a bench at her side.

Lisa asked, "Have you seen Jim?"

"No."

"Who's this?"

"One of those goddesses. Artemis, maybe. Bow and arrow—is that right? I didn't pay much attention in school. Most of the time I was bored stiff. Couldn't wait to get out and see the world."

"I loved it," she said.

"Sit down."

"I just came out to find Jim. We're leaving."

"I thought you were staying till Monday. I hoped you were. Don't go."

"We really have to," she told him, walking away.

He got up and fell into step beside her. He said, "Tonight and tomorrow are the best times. People come from all around. It's when we hold the séances."

"Oh, God," she said. In the distance Jim was walking toward them. He raised a hand. "There he is. I'll just have a couple of words with him." She hurried ahead.

"We're staying," he said.

"Jim, I can't stand another minute in this place."

"Every time I turn around, you look like you're having a great time with that Farley Granger clone."

"Last night I was nearly raped by four men while you were getting a drink of water."

"Last night you were completely pie-eyed and suffering from massive wish fulfillment."

"Oh Jesus, how can you be so stupid? How—"

"We're leaving right after dinner, but if it's too late, then we'll go in the morning. Whatever happens, we're definitely staying till the late evening, because Henry Kissinger's invited."

"Who?"

"Ex–Secretary of State, Kissinger, a name you may have seen in the papers?"

"What are you talking about?"

"He's coming here for dinner tonight."

"Why?"

"Christ. Because he was asked, of course."

"Well. Well, so what?"

"Look, Lisa: I see nothing wrong about name-dropping, and if I get a chance to sit at the same table with a name like Kissinger, a part of American history, I'm sure as hell not going to miss it. Are you? Isabelle says he tells wonderful stories. Come on, Lisa, are you with me or what?"

"Give me the keys," she said.

"Keys?"

"I'll drive back, and you can get a ride with Henry Kissinger or somebody else."

"Of course not. It would be unforgivably rude."

"I don't believe he's coming."

"He is."

"I'll make a scene."

"Hah."

"I'll say I recognize him from photographs as the Nazi commandant of a concentration camp. I'll—"

"Lisa," he said, "you just shut up and be nice. It's been a little strange, but you're going to have to take it. I've got an important deal on with Broderick and if you mess things up, believe me you're going to be sorry, because I won't stand for it."

He'd never spoken to her like that. She felt her whole body, and especially her face, go rigid with fury and desperation. She wheeled around and ran off across the lawn.

She reached the front drive and slowed down. It wasn't yet noon, the sun was bright; she could walk through all the country roads until afternoon, and by that time she'd hit the highway and find help. She'd phone the police or the Automobile Association, or a friend from town, to come get her.

She settled into a regular stride. It wasn't going to be easy in her party shoes, though they weren't too high and so far felt comfortable. Her lips moved but she wasn't actually muttering. She was thinking about all the times he'd been in the wrong and unfair to her—how this was really the limit and it would serve him right.

She plowed through a muddy field of deep grass and came out onto the driveway. It took her a lot longer than she'd expected to reach the road. Everything looked different in the daytime. In fact, it all looked beautiful. If the house hadn't been such a perfect replica of Haunted House Gothic, the setting could equally well have accommodated a fairy-tale palace. Everywhere she looked there was a superabundance of blossoming hedges, gnarled trees, mossy banks and starry flowers. She began to feel stronger as she went on, despite the shoes: a long walk over stony and uneven ground wasn't going to do them any good—she could tell that already. They'be ruined afterward for anything but rainy days.

She hummed a little. She reached the road and stopped, looking from left to right and rubbing her hands. She realized suddenly that she'd been scratching at her hands for a long while, trying to get rid of an itch in the folds between her fingers. She'd made all the itchy places bright pink. Red spots like the beginnings of a rash had come up between two of the fingers on her left hand. Nerves, she thought; or possibly a reaction to the peculiar food from the night before.

She turned to the left. For five minutes she walked without seeing a car or a person. Then ahead, coming toward her from around the next corner, she saw two men: rough-looking, bearded and wearing dungarees. She felt apprehensive straightaway. She wanted to turn around and go back. Should she look at them, or past them; say hello, or what? What could she do to make them walk on and not take any notice of her?

One was short, the other tall. They didn't look right at her as they went by, but they were fooling. Almost as soon as she'd passed they were back again, one on each side of her, walking in her direction and near enough, if they wanted to, to grab her arms.

"Looking for something, girlie?" the short one said.

"No thanks, I'm fine," she answered in a small, tight, terrified voice that made her even more frightened.

"Well, we'll just walk along with you a ways," the big one said. "Keep you from getting lonely. Just in case something was to happen to a nice little girl like you."

She looked up quickly. They were both grinning. Would they just terrorize her, or did they mean to act? Maybe they'd kill her afterward, so she couldn't identify them. Maybe they meant to kill her anyway, just for fun. She'd never be able to run fast enough. It was probably better to give in as soon as possible and die quickly. If she were strong, at least she'd be able to hurt them back somehow.

The little one was beginning to jostle her. They were ready to start; pretty soon his friend would be doing it too. She stepped back and to the side, saying, "Well, if nobody's going to leave me alone today, I might as well go back to my friends. They were right behind me." She began to walk back, in the direction of the house.

They turned and came with her.

"Now isn't that a shame?" the tall one said. "She doesn't like our company."

"That really hurts my feelings," the short one told him.

She was itchy and sore all over now. It was difficult to keep walking.

"You think she meant to be mean like that?" the small one asked. "You think she's one of those stuck-up bitches that takes it out on you?"

"I think maybe that's just what she is," the big one said. "I met plenty like her. I know her type."

Her pulse was drumming in her throat and the hairs rising

on her arms. Surely it wouldn't happen. It couldn't happen, because she was having such a hard time simply continuing to breathe that long before they started to drag her across the road, she'd have a heart attack. She hoped she'd have one— that everything would just stop all of a sudden and be no more.

She took her eyes from the surface of the road and looked toward the turning. In front of her, emerging from a thicket of bushes to the left, were two people who waved. "There they are," she called out, and sprinted ahead. She could run after all. But she stopped when she was a few yards away. It hadn't occurred to her that she might really know the couple. Now she recognized them: it was Dora and Steve.

"Friends of yours?" Steve said.

"I never saw them before." She turned and looked back. The two men were gone.

"I didn't think they looked very trustworthy," Dora said. "This is a lonely road. You'd better come on back with us."

"So, you're a friend of nature, too?"Steve asked. He had a notebook and ballpoint pen in his hand, field glasses hanging from a strap around his neck. "This is wonderful country for it. Best in the world. That's the other reason we keep coming here."

"I can't stay," Lisa told him. "We were only coming for supper last night, that's all. I've got to get back. For private reasons. And now Jim won't even let me go by myself. But that's silly. It isn't fair. I was trying to walk it."

"In those shoes?" Dora said. "Oh dear."

"You have a car here, don't you? Could you drive me? Just to a bus stop or a train station?" She scratched violently at her hands.

"You've got that chlorine reaction, too," Dora said. "I've got an ointment I can lend you."

"I just want to get home," Lisa wailed.

"But you wouldn't want to miss the party. You know who's going to be here tonight, don't you?"

"This is important. It's a family matter. Couldn't you?"

"All right," Steve said. "Of course. Right after lunch. Just let us finish the notes first, otherwise we'll have to start all over again. That's soon enough, isn't it—say, just before three? I'd make it earlier, but this is a working weekend as well as pleasure. We're compiling a book—did I tell you?"

"Oh?"

"Toads."

"Dear little things," Dora said. "And fascinating."

"You could stay indoors and do all the research you need," Lisa said. "They're in the house, too."

"What do you mean?"

"In the upstairs bathroom, in the shower. There was a whole nest, a big pile of them. Last night."

"Don't tell me they got out?" Steve said.

"It must be another batch," Dora told him. "Ours were fine this morning. I guess you're lucky they didn't nip your toes when you were stepping in there. They're carnivorous, you know." She laughed in hearty barks that ended in a whoop of amusement.

Lisa said. "Thanks for telling me."

They came in sight of the house. Dora said she'd go get that tube of medicine, and added that she couldn't believe Lisa was really going to run off and miss the opportunity of meeting Henry Kissinger. They walked around the terrace to the far side, passing as they went a line of large, brand-new and expensive cars parked against the balustrade. Steve said the cars belonged to patients.

"You'd be surprised," he told Lisa, "how many people consult Broderick and Isabelle. In all walks of life, too: movie stars, politicians, big businessmen—you name it."

"Kissinger?"

"I think he's just an ordinary guest."

"Norman Mailer was here last weekend," Dora said. "He talked for hours about glands."

"Hormones," her husband corrected.

"And Henry Fonda before that."

"He's dead," Lisa said.

"Well, maybe it was the other one."

"Which other one? The son?"

"Gary Cooper. Or was it John Wayne?"

"I think we're getting all these names a little mixed up," Steve explained. He winked at Lisa.

"Anyway," Dora said, "he was very nice."

They had a cold lunch of food that once again, like the breakfast, was good: salads with chicken, ham and beef; fruit and ice cream afterward. The coffee looked all right too, but Lisa didn't want to try it.

Jim wouldn't look at her. She heard a long account from Dr. Benjamin about tree frogs in Africa. He examined her hands and told her there was nothing to worry about: all the redness was simply a result of friction. As she listened, she could see Carrol, only four seats away, scratching and rubbing herself, touching her face all the time.

She said to the doctor, "Steve and Dora are giving me a ride back to town at three, but I'm in kind of a hurry. I'd like to get away sooner than that. Did you come by car?"

"I came with them," he told her. "And I think Broderick picked the two girls up on his way out from town. Why don't you ask him? I'm sure he'd run you in."

"I'd hate to bother him," she said. "We'll see."

She went upstairs to wait till three. She paced all around the bed, looking carefully at the dark edging of the heavy, brocaded spread. She sat down on top of it, inspected the material and then slowly prepared to curl up. She lowered her head, but she kept her shoes on. She slept for a few minutes, waking up in a rush as soon as she heard someone walking down the hall.

Jim opened the door, shut it behind him and came over to her. He said, "What's wrong with you?"

"I want to go home. Please, Jim. Remember the food last night?"

"It was fine just now."

"And the cold, and the smell. Those animals in the shower. And I mean it about what happened when you left. You don't believe me, but you don't believe anything from me anymore."

"I'm not staying here for an accusation session."

"Just let me have the car keys, for God's sake. What difference is it going to make to you?"

"If you walk out of here, if you're rude, if you make a scene—it makes me look bad."

"No, it doesn't. I act on my own."

"You're here with me."

"I tried to leave. I was going to walk. Look at my shoes. Two guys on the road tried to grab me."

"Uh-huh. Guys trying to grab you every time you turn around."

"Just let me get out, Jim. Please."

"We're leaving Monday morning."

"Monday? This is only Saturday."

"We've been invited for the weekend."

"Well, if this is even the right house, it was only supposed to be supper on Friday. I don't have a change of underpants or anything. Neither do you."

"Isabelle says she can let you have whatever you like."

"What I'd like is to get back to town."

They argued back and forth in a normal tone at first, then in whispers, and nearly shouting. He wanted to know how she could be so parochial as to leave just when Henry Kissinger was about to arrive: wasn't she interested in world politics, in history?

She said, "You don't believe he's really coming here, do you? To eat mud soup and old tires? Him and Norman Mailer and John Wayne and all the rest of them? They just want to get us to stay here, that's all."

"Why?"

"I don't know. They just do."

"You mean, they're telling us lies?"

"Of course they are."

"But why would they do that?"

"Because they want us to stay."

"It doesn't make sense."

"Does any of it? Look at me." She held out her hands. The skin was patched with pink lumps. "Look at my hands," she told him.

"What have you done to them?"

"I haven't done anything. They're itching because of something in this house."

"Oh, Lisa. I don't know what's gotten into you. Try to calm down."

She stood up. "Right," she said. "Steve and Dora can give me a ride. And now I know how much I'd be able to count on you." She snatched up her purse and looked at her wristwatch. It said four-thirty. "God, I'm late. Oh, God."

"That settles it."

"Yes. I'll see if they'll still do it. And if they won't, you'll have to."

"Nope."

"And if you don't, we're through."

"That's up to you. You're going to feel pretty foolish when you look back and see how unreasonable you're being."

"And I'm calling the police."

He stood up and threw her back onto the bed. "Everything you want," he hissed at her. "Always for you and never for the both of us, never for me. Who's going to have to build up a career and pay off the mortgage and all the rest of it, hm? You won't cook for my friends, you won't do this or that—"

"And what about you?" she screeched. "Leave me there with a list of all the errands I've got to run for you: I've got a job too, you know. You're a grown man. You can wash your own goddamn socks once in a while."

"You aren't going to give me that women's lib stuff, are you?"

"Just this once—just get me out of here and I'll do anything. You can come straight back, if you like. Please."

"Don't cry like that. Somebody could hear you."

"Please."

"All right," he said.

She sprang toward the door. He followed slowly. They went down the stairs together, Lisa running ahead.

Isabelle was standing at the foot of the staircase. She was dressed in another long, dark robe and her hair was even more elaborately arranged than on the night before. This time the string of pearls that twined through the pile of stacked braids included a single jewel; it hung from the center parting onto her forehead. It looked like a ruby, surrounded by tiny pearls. "And where are you two off to?" she asked.

Lisa said, "I'm sorry, Isabelle—I really am. It's been so lovely here, but we left town thinking it was just for supper last night. I had three people I was supposed to see today, and now I've got to go—I've really got to. The others are going to be furious. I'll have to patch that up somehow, but my mother"—her voice quivered. "My mother's operation comes first. I've just got to get back. We should have said straightaway. Jim—"she turned to him; he could do some worrying for a change, after putting her through all this: "Jim thought you'd be upset if we refused your hospitality. I was sure you'd understand. He can stay, of course. But my mother can't wait, I'm afraid. Not even for Mr. Kissinger."

"That's another disappointment. He just called. He can't make it tonight. Maybe tomorrow, he said. Such a shame. We look forward to his visits so much."

"Tomorrow?" Jim repeated. He sounded hopeful.

"Not for me," Lisa insisted.

Broderick had appeared at the end of the corridor, the other guests grouped behind him. He began to lead them all down the carpet toward the staircase and the light. "What's this?" he said.

"Lisa wants to leave us," Isabelle told him.

"I don't want to. I've got to, that's all. My mother's having a serious operation."

"When?" Broderick asked.

"On Friday afternoon they told me it was going to be tonight, possibly tomorrow morning. I've got to get back."

"I can drive you," Broderick offered.

"Thanks, but Jim's going to."

"I know the roads around here. And I'm used to the fog. Have you seen what it's like?"

"We waited for you," Steve complained. Dora, beside him, asked, "Where were you? You said three."

"I couldn't find you," Lisa said. She suddenly didn't believe that they had waited, or that Henry Kissinger had ever been on the guest list, or that she was going to be allowed out of the house, which was definitely the wrong house. She put her hand on Jim's arm. Her fingers, her whole arm, trembled.

"Why don't you phone the hospital?" Isabelle suggested. She picked up the receiver from the telephone on the table next to her.

They were going to try to fake her out, Lisa thought. But she could phone a taxi, or even the police, if she wanted to. Or—a better idea—a friend: Broderick was undoubtedly on good terms with all the lawyers, doctors and policemen in the neighborhood, as well as any local politicians who lived nearby. "That's a good idea," she said. She let go of Jim's arm and came down the last few stairs.

Isabelle put her ear to the receiver. She said, "Well, wouldn't you know it? It does this sometimes in a thick fog. It's gone completely dead."

Me, too, Lisa thought. She turned to Jim and said, "I mean it. Now."

He spread his hands toward Isabelle. "I'm really sorry," he said.

"Another time," she told him. She shook his hand and smiled. She shook Lisa's hand too, holding the friendly look and the smile.

Broderick called after them, "Come on back if the fog catches up with you. They can be dangerous. People can actually choke to death in them."

All the air outdoors was smoky. They got into the car. Lisa said nothing, although she felt safe already. If they had to, she wouldn't mind sleeping in the backseat. At least they'd be away from the house. Jim turned the key. He drove the car across the gravel. Lisa waved at the dimly lighted doorway.

They moved down the drive, along the woodland road and out onto the highway, where almost immediately they hit the real fog. Jim went very slowly. The fog came toward them in long strips like white veiling that kept tearing in pieces or bunching up around them.

"What was all that about your mother?" he said.

"I had to think of something they couldn't explain away. It would have looked bad if they hadn't been sympathetic."

"Isabelle was very nice about it."

"She was mad as hell."

"She was not. She was kind and understanding."

"And she has Kissinger for dinner just all the time—oh, yes. And what a surprise: the phone doesn't work."

"What are you getting at?"

"Those weirdo people holding occult meetings together."

"They're wonderful people. They're studying phenomena that can't be explained yet by any of the scientific principles we know of so far. How do you think anyone ever gets to know things, anyway? There's always a time when it sounds crazy and crackpot—when it's all being tried out experimentally. As soon as a thing's accepted, then it's considered normal."

"You think that house is normal?"

"Well, the heating's kind of erratic and the pipes don't work so well, and what do you expect? It's a big old place down in the country. It'd cost a fortune to fix it up."

"It wouldn't cost a fortune to give us tuna salad to eat, instead of whatever that horrible stuff was. It wouldn't—"

"Wait," he said. All the windows had suddenly gone stark white. The effect was blinding until he turned off the lights. He slowed the car to a crawl. "If it gets any worse, you'll have to walk in front, to show me where the edge of the road is."

"No. We can just stop here and sleep in the car. Pull off the road."

"You heard what Broderick said about the fog."

"I don't believe it."

"Well, I do."

"I'm not going back there, Jim," she said.

"Jesus Christ," he shouted, "what's wrong with you?" He stopped the car and switched off the ignition. "I think you're crazy," he said. "I really do. Just like your whole damn family."

"OK. You can think what you like, as long as we never have to go back to that place."

"This is the end of us, you know. I can't go on with you after this."

"If we just get home, we'll be all right."

"You screwed up everything with them. I don't know how anybody could have behaved the way you did. Completely hysterical, and lying your head off. It was obvious."

"But does that mean I've got to die for it?"

"Die? Nobody's going to die."

"And why do we have to split up? Why do they mean more to you than I do? You didn't even know them before yesterday."

"I guess maybe I didn't know you very well, either."

"Oh, shove that."

"Uh-huh. Nice."

"You know me. And you know how I feel about you."

"Maybe not." He opened his window a crack. They could see the white fog creep in like smoke. He tried the lights again. This time the glare wasn't thrown back, but the lights didn't seem to penetrate more than a few feet into the shifting areas of blankness.

She said, "When you got up for that drink of water last night, where did you go?"

"Down the hall to the bathroom."

"You were with somebody else, weren't you?"

"No," he said. "But it's a good idea."

The whiteness became all-enveloping. The temperature began to drop inside the car. The sound of rain seemed to be coming from somewhere, though they couldn't see any.

"I don't understand," she said, "how you could have let us get into all that."

"It was too foggy to drive back. It was like this."

"And this morning, when I asked you for the keys?"

"This morning you were already crazy; people grabbing you left and right. If this doesn't clear soon—"

"We sit it out."

"I suppose so." He was about to cut the lights, when something dark thudded against the windshield and was gone again.

"A bat," Lisa called out.

"No. It didn't look . . . I think it was rounder. Maybe a bird. I guess the light attracted it."

There was another sound as two more of the things struck Lisa's side window. She undid her seat belt and moved near to Jim.

He was watching the glass in front of him. Several more of the dark shapes hit. They sounded like rubber balls being thrown against the car, all over the metal parts suddenly: on the roof, too. He leaned forward. "Frogs," he said. They were everywhere, bouncing up and down, lying still, or slithering across the glass.

"Not frogs," Lisa moaned. "Toads."

"Jesus, will you look at them—there must be hundreds."

"Thousands," she said. "Oh, my God."

He turned off the lights. It didn't have any effect. The toads continued to bombard the car.

"Maybe if we start moving again," he said.

"We can't. They're jamming themselves into the exhaust. Can't you hear them?"

"I could really step on it and blow the muffler off." He switched the engine on again, turned the lights high.

Now the toads were all over. They blocked the view from the windows. They were also a great deal bigger than before. When one of them landed, it sounded like a soccer ball.

He started to drive. The exhaust pipe roared, the car inched forward. He tried to use the windshield wipers, but the toads hung on until the blades stuck in one position. There were swarms of the animals, uncountable. Clusters of them lay squashed or flattened on the windows. And the big ones crashed down on top of them. A dark liquid began to run over the panes.

"Could they break the glass?" she asked.

"I don't know. It's safety glass. They might be able to bang into it hard enough, if they all jumped together."

"They're carnivorous," she said.

AN ARTIST'S LIFE

Axel and Eino met only because one morning Axel turned his head; he'd heard the cry of a bird—a seabird of some kind. The wind whipped into his face and he pulled down his hat. At that moment he saw ahead of him on the bridge a young man, walking toward him, who made a similar gesture and then put up his other hand to adjust a scarf around his throat.

The next day at about the same time Axel caught sight of the man at a different spot, this time beyond the bridge; he was hurrying forward, his head down so that it was impossible to see his face, but Axel recognized the clothes he was wearing, which were copied from the bohemian Paris of earlier decades.

Axel, whose family was more than three-quarters Swedish and had money and houses and land, wore French and English clothes of good quality and cut. He might have been mistaken for a Parisian. He was tall, gray-eyed and brown-haired. He had the languid demeanor—in fashion at the time—supposed to denote good breeding; among those who adopted it, at any rate, the attitude was a sign that they thought so.

Eino was of a different stamp: very blond, round-headed and burly. He walked quickly, with a jerky, bobbing gait. He held the upper part of his body—shoulders, back and arms— like a man who was strong. On the first day Axel saw his face, Eino looked ready to kill someone. He must have been cold as he turned against the wind.

On the third day, Axel saw him after crossing the bridge. Eino was searching the gutter for something. Once more he had his head down and Axel noticed the clothes.

He didn't see Eino for a while after that and when he did, he heard him first: he heard a voice saying in Finnish, "Do they think we're idiots?" and he stopped.

He looked around. The man who had made the remark was standing with his back toward Axel; he had his hands in his pockets and was shifting quickly from one foot to the other. He was examining the objects in a shop window. The awning above protected him from the light drizzle that had begun to fall. Axel had his umbrella.

He knew that he'd seen the stranger before, although he hadn't thought the man would be a fellow countryman. He walked up to the shop window and stood beside Eino, to look at a large, pink ostrich feather and a set of stands stacked with jars of cosmetic cream. Ribbons had been made to cascade from top to bottom of the display, so that the separate groupings seemed like bouquets of flowers. Several colored sketches of young women illustrated the beneficial properties of the ointment.

"Who do they think they're fooling?" Eino muttered. "If the woman's good-looking, she doesn't need anything."

"And if she isn't," Axel said, "it wouldn't help her."

"Exactly. Women like that must be weak in the head."

"They have hope. They might start to look better because they're in a good mood."

"But the stuff is worthless."

"Of course."

"Half the damn things you see in shop windows are worthless."

"But—they sell."

"Because people are fools."

"The ones who buy, perhaps. What about the ones who sell?"

Eino laughed. "Swindlers. All of them."

"It can't be that bad."

"It's worse."

Axel moved away. He was far down the street and thinking of other things when he was pulled from behind. He whirled around, to find himself staring at Eino, who said, "You were speaking Finnish. I didn't realize. Talk to me. Talk to me in Finnish."

Axel repositioned his umbrella. The man looked desperate as well as poor, but was about his own age, which—at his age—seemed to make him all right. "We'll go to a café," he suggested.

"I don't have any money."

"I think I've got enough to buy you a beer."

"No," Eino told him. "We'll walk."

Axel agreed. He went as far as the café on the street corner across from the park and then said, "If it were better weather, we could sit here, but as it is, I'm finding it difficult to keep in step with a man who doesn't have an umbrella. If you won't come into the café and let me buy you a drink, I'll say goodbye."

They went in together. Axel ordered tea and biscuits. Eino drank coffee. There were four other men in the room, all old and all reading the papers.

"I've walked by this place plenty of times," Eino said, "and never gone in. I've never even wondered what it was like inside."

"There must be thousands of cafés in this part of town."

"I love big cities. You never get to the end of them. Every street has a row of new places you've never explored."

"The whole world is like that," Axel said.

"Some of it. Not the part I grew up in. Not Finland. You grew up in town, didn't you?"

"Oh, nothing like this. A small university town in Sweden, a village in Finland; a few summers in St. Petersburg when my grandparents were alive—that was the nearest I got, but I was still a child then. Paris was always my dream."

"Has it lived up to what you expected of it?"

"Yes, completely," Axel said.

At the beginning it had been even better than the expectation, except in one important respect, but he didn't know Eino well enough to talk about that: it hadn't fulfilled his hopes for the erotic, as well as the romantic, life. He'd imagined that it would be simple to meet women who were easy to ask, but so far he'd managed to find only the places where all the girls were too obviously professional, and that still made him a little nervous.

He'd had two affairs with girls down in the country and one with a scandalous young woman who'd said she was getting a divorce from her elderly husband: that one had been the most fun. It had lasted throughout the summer and ended because Axel had made a scene when he'd found out that he wasn't the only man she was seeing. She'd screamed at him that he was unsophisticated. And the next week, when he'd gone back to apologize, she'd laughed at him while the maid stood by the door, holding his coat and listening to everything. After that, he'd had a steady, once-a-week meeting with a married woman in her late thirties: Martha. She'd been in love with him. For him the meetings had been merely a convenience—he was always looking for someone else. But for her they became the center of life and she couldn't help showing it. As she kept wanting more of him, he retreated. By the time he broke it off, he could barely stand to be near her. He didn't even care that— as he'd once feared—she might try to commit suicide.

He saw her in town on three different occasions after the break; once at a concert, when she didn't realize he was standing at the back of the room. She had the look of a woman who was dying.

She'd written letters to his mother, pleading that he be allowed to see her. That had been his fault: rather than saying outright that he didn't love her, he'd invented a story in which his parents' views played a ruling part. *A married woman*, he'd said: they'd be horrified.

Axel's mother was indeed horrified. She couldn't understand why, instead of asking his father for advice about these things, he'd implicated a decent, married woman in his philanderings; and evidently hurt her very deeply. But, Axel had answered, his father's advice had been to get married as soon as possible to a rich girl with no looks, who would bring him enough money for a comfortable life and would always do what he told her. His mother wasn't too happy about that reply. Over the next few days his father came into the argument too, and it was eventually decided that if Axel agreed to take a job working with Thorvaldsen's cousin at the bank, they'd let him go to Paris for a year, as he'd always wanted—to see if he could become a painter.

He'd been there since October. And now it was January.

"And you?" he asked Eino. "How do you come to be so far from home? Did you always dream about living in Paris?"

"Not at first. In the beginning I just wanted to go away, anywhere. I couldn't get along with them at home. And I hated school."

"I liked school, but I was lucky. I had good teachers and tutors."

"It doesn't depend on the teachers. I just didn't have the aptitude for it. Otherwise . . . What I wanted to do was to be an architect, or something along those lines—to make things and to build them. I was always good with my hands. I had a great-uncle like that; he'd sit all day long, whittling things with a penknife: animals, people—he could do anything. He taught me to paint, to draw; to hunt, and do woodcarving. For that kind of thing I loved being in the country. And for real work—to do hard work that satisfies your body. I helped a friend of my father's to build a house once. That was fine. That was a side of home life that I liked."

"Me too," Axel said. All his life he'd felt comforted and healed by the beauty of the countryside, although as far as any real work went, they'd had servants for that.

"In the town," Eino told him, "you just sit on a stool and don't do anything, and you're ready to die of tiredness at the end of the day. It isn't healthy."

"You mean school?"

"School, and most businesses. My aunts had a confectionery shop—a big place, staff, everything tied up in ribbons and fancy wrapping, people making the boxes, importing ingredients, and so on. When I was a boy they let me design the boxes."

"And all the chocolate you could eat, I suppose."

"They say it's poison, you know—all sweet food: that it rots your insides, not just your teeth."

"The favorite food of children."

"Yes. Right from the beginning we develop a taste for what's going to destroy us."

"Well," Axel said, "that's putting it rather strongly. If you live long enough, you can die of anything. It's simply a matter of time, isn't it?"

Eino laughed. Tears came to his eyes. The laughter began to sound wild. It made Axel wonder if he was sick or crazy, or even hungrier than he'd assumed. "But the chocolate wasn't enough?" he said.

"I'd been taken to a museum once. My mother wanted to look at china—plates and vases, that sort of thing. And they had a section for Venetian glass. That made a big impression on me. I wanted to know how it was possible to form a hard material like that into shapes—to add color to it, to make a glass flower or even a glass bowl. Then they told me that the men who made things out of glass did it by blowing molten bubbles. Of course I thought that was wonderful. I wanted to see it straightaway. I kept asking to go. You know, I'd forgotten all this. It's odd how things suddenly pop into your head when you get to talking. That's right: I made them take me to a glass factory somewhere. As a matter of fact, I don't remember too much about that. It wasn't very interesting after all. The next craze was wanting to learn about architecture. That wasn't any good. I couldn't do the schoolwork. But I always had this idea that I'd build a house—a real one. Big. Not just helping to work on somebody's summer cabin. I still think so. There are plenty of good houses that were built without mathematics, aren't there?"

"Of course," Axel said, although he had an idea that the big houses usually demanded a preliminary plan and a lot of calculation—measurements, investigation of the surrounding land, information about soil and drainage.

Eino said, "My father always wanted a boat, all his life. He had the idea, but it was only a wish on his part. He never had the absolute certainty that one day he'd get the boat. But in my case, you see, I just know I'm going to build that house."

"And that's why you came to Paris, to learn about—"

"No, that was a long time ago. What happened was that they sent me to Berlin to learn about the restaurant trade and I wanted to be a painter, so I just jumped on the first train out. A friend of mine came with me, but he moved on. I stayed put, and painted."

"You're a painter?" It didn't seem possible to Axel that anyone his own age, anyone from his own country, and especially anyone he knew, could be a genuine painter. "That's how you make your living?"

"If you can call it that. I do a lot of other things, too. Anything for cash."

"Portraits?"

"Portraits, landscapes, billboards, valentines, playbills, ceilings. And you? You don't have to work, am I right?"

"I work in a bank."

"I see. That explains it."

"What?"

"The clothes."

"It's only like any other uniform." He smiled, thinking that Eino too was dressed in a kind of uniform; some looks were chosen, some imposed according to someone else's choice. He wasn't ready to say that he too was a painter, that he wasn't getting anywhere with it, and that after discovering how inferior all his work was, he wasn't enjoying it any longer.

He'd realized just before Christmas. The knowledge had ruined his holiday. He'd come in late after the office celebrations, sat down at his writing table, opened the presents from his family, and suddenly felt so homesick that he'd wanted to weep. There were books, and some extra money from his parents, cards and letters from aunts and uncles and cousins; a scarf his sister, Anna, had knitted for him, a pair of opera glasses from his uncle Karl, a photograph of all the family gathered together. And he'd given up all that family life for the sake of the dismal, misshapen daubs propped against the wall in front of him and beside the chair in the corner. He could see all at once that in putting the paint on the canvas he had been responsible for adding to the ugliness in the world. It would have been better if those objects had never been made. Nor was he a success, as he'd dreamed, in any other way. He was in the capital city of love, and was ready to die of loneliness.

"I couldn't work in a bank," Eino said.

"Why not?"

"The routine would kill me."

"It's actually full of variety. They keep moving you around

from one department to another. It's quite interesting. Very interesting, really—only I always wanted to do something more, ah, artistic."

"And the fixed hours. Once you've been your own boss, every other kind of job seems servile."

"I don't look at it that way. You can't get anything much done without a certain amount of teamwork and cooperation."

"Would you rather be the one giving the orders, or carrying them out?"

"I don't think it matters, as long as the work is important. Of course, I'm not like you—I was never very good with my hands, so there are some jobs I'd rather not try. I was better at all the mathematics and sitting at a desk."

"I could only work for somebody I liked."

"Most people feel like that."

"Most people don't have the choice. They're glad to get any kind of work."

"Do you go back for visits?"

"No. I write to one of my sisters, once in a while. Do you?"

"I've only been here a few months. But I write to them, all the time. They'd be worried if I missed a week. I expect your family believes in more independence."

"We had a big fight," Eino said. "I haven't seen any of them for three years." He put down his empty cup and breathed out. He was about to say thanks for the coffee.

Axel asked, "Do you think I could see your paintings sometime?"

When he looked around the walls at Eino's pictures, Axel knew for certain that he himself stood no chance of becoming a painter, even if he were to start all over again. Eino painted easily and quickly. The canvases hung around the room and leaning in rows against the walls were clear, bright, attractive. Even if they weren't great, they were well presented. Axel liked them.

He also liked, and was extremely impressed by, the way Eino lived. They were the same age, yet Eino had dared to step straight into the bohemian life: he had a mistress named Marissa and a small child—a boy called Bruno—who was dark-eyed, like his mother.

Marissa approved of Axel immediately. His presence in their circle seemed to her an indication that Eino might soon work his way toward the respectability she longed for. She invited Axel to come see them whenever he liked.

He took to visiting them early in the evening, or—at the end of the week—in the late afternoon. If the weather was good, he'd stroll to a café with them and buy them all something to drink. If it was raining, they stayed at home; he might bring cakes with him, or flowers. One afternoon, at the beginning of their acquaintance, Axel came to call and found that Eino was out. He was embarrassed and said he wouldn't stay, but Marissa told him that he had to come in and sit down—she wanted to talk to him.

He sat on a chair while she brought out the bath for the child. She wouldn't let him help her with anything. "You just sit there," she ordered. "You don't know how nice it is to have someone to talk to. Sometimes I'm so lonely, I start talking to myself. And I know where he is, too. He's with that woman. I suppose you know who I mean."

"No," Axel said. "Who?"

"There's no need for you to try to protect him."

"I don't know who you mean. You're the only woman Eino has introduced me to."

"A rich woman who's got a studio full of other rich women. They're all trying to be painters and sculptors. I call it the Marie Antoinette club. She's in love with Eino."

"But he loves you."

"Then why doesn't he marry me?" she asked. The child shrieked as she began to undress it.

"Maybe he doesn't believe in the institution of marriage."

"Men just say those things. It means it makes it easier to leave."

"He wouldn't leave a woman with a child? Surely not."

"And another one coming," she muttered. "I was a fool. I didn't want to lose him. I loved him too much." She tugged at the child's arm and hissed, "Be quiet," into its screaming

face. She didn't look like a woman who had ever loved
anyone.

As he got to know Eino better, Axel met a good many people,
most of them women. He began to assume things that Eino
didn't tell him. He suspected, for example, that Eino was
sleeping with the wife of the grocer down at the end of the
street, and with a widow who occasionally hired him to do
painting and repairs in her daughter's house; and with a few
others. The woman whom Marissa thought of as the guilty
one was—according to Eino—not on his list.

Axel met her one rainy day just before afternoon turned
into evening. Rain poured down the high windows of her
studio. She'd had the fires lit in the drawing room and was
about to pull the curtains. Everything in the room was plump
and lustrous: the velvet cushions, the thick, plush sofa
covers, brocade curtains: even the figured wallpaper. But the
studio beyond was plain. The far wall was simple plaster, the
doorframe in it unpainted and the floorboards bare. Three
women were at work under the vaulted, glass-paned roof;
they wore aprons like shopkeepers or butchers and had their
hair pinned back severely. It seemed to Axel at first sight that
they were like the three daughters of a fairy tale: old, middle
and young. The old one was an American spinster who
painted badly but enthusiastically; the middle woman was
good-looking—the young wife of an older man; a manufac-
turer of some kind, who was proud of her accomplishments.
And the youngest was a black-haired German girl named
Minna. She was very young: a large girl, not especially pretty,
but she had something; as soon as you noticed that she was
fairly plain, you decided she had a certain charm that made
up for that. Her subject was sculpture. She was modeling a
bust in clay when Axel was introduced to her. He nodded
and smiled. At that moment he was more interested in the
founder of the school and owner of the house, who showed
them back to the warmer room and rang for tea.

"They stay on late, even when the weather's like this," she
said.

"Karen never has a free moment," Eino explained.

"All my moments are free, my dear," she told him. "That's why you're never going to get anywhere with all that. Stop pushing and sit down." She dropped into a chair and laughed. Axel and Eino took the chairs set in front of her, so she could see them both without turning her head. The positioning was a little like the seating in a small boat.

He began to forget about everything else as she talked. He thought he was falling in love with her: with the look of her clear skin and the pale color of her hair; with her voice, her thoughts, the serenity of her manner and irony of her speech. He said so to Eino afterward while they were walking through the rain. But Eino told him, "No, it's just friendship. I thought the same thing myself at first, but you'll see: she isn't for love."

"Of course she is. She's wonderful."

"Oh, I agree. And she's beautiful too, but she's rather—not alluring, you know. She's like a nursemaid. One doesn't have romantic thoughts about her."

"Speak for yourself. I think she's lovely."

"Everything about her is so nice and tidy. All in its place, so controlled."

"Yes. I admire that."

"And—I'm not sure how much she likes men."

"She likes you. I got the impression she liked me, too."

"That wasn't what I meant. I think somehow she doesn't take certain things seriously. Anything much, really. Certainly not love."

"You were flirting with her all the time."

"I like her a lot. It aggravates me that she's never going to say yes."

"So, she never has lovers? She's always been alone?"

"Well, that's the mystery. You think you've understood the way it is, and then suddenly there are these intriguing flashes of something else, and you wonder."

"Tell me some more about her."

Eino talked about Karen—what he knew about her family back in Sweden, and of her friends in Paris. The school, he said, had been going for six years and was a success, although it hadn't yet produced any outstanding work.

"And Karen herself?"

"She's a good painter. Nothing she ever does is bad or cheap or a poor imitation. But she doesn't have the eye. She doesn't see in a new way, or make a shape or a vision that seems to be a new form. She's a little better than I am, that's all."

"But you're good."

"I'm competent, yes. And that's good. But there are gradations, and you asked me. A really important school of art would be turning out students who broke the mold. Maybe not in six years, of course."

"I don't understand," Axel said, "how you can talk about art like this, when you can paint the way you do."

"That's why. I'm a practitioner. You're an appreciator."

"Well, as far as that goes, someday if we get really drunk together, I'll show you my paintings."

"You?"

"I think there are a few left that I haven't painted over."

"What's wrong with now?" Eino said.

"There isn't enough time. We'd have to be drinking all day."

"We'll make up for it in speed," Eino told him.

They went out drinking for three hours. Axel still didn't want to show Eino the paintings. "You'll think I'm such a fool," he said. "I wish now I'd never mentioned them. You'll see them, and you'll think: *how could this man be a friend of mine?*"

"Axel, if you don't show them to me tonight, I'll know you didn't trust me enough. And if you don't show them to me now, I'm going to be too drunk to see them. Come on." Eino rose from his seat and plunged out into the night, dragging Axel after him. Axel tried to get his hand free in order to put up his umbrella, but Eino wouldn't listen to his complaints. They were both soaked to the skin.

Axel led the way upstairs, trudging ahead slowly. Eino prodded him from behind. "Don't make so much noise," Axel told him. "You'll get me thrown out."

"What for? You pay your rent, don't you? Besides, I can find you a better place than this."

They reached the top. Axel struggled with the key, threw open the door and fumbled his way across the room. "Heat and light," he said. "I want you to feel comfortable when you start to laugh."

Eino said nothing. He stood near the door until Axel had everything prepared, and then looked at the paintings as they were thrust forward.

Axel did all the talking. He said, "Oh God, they're so terrible, oh God. They're awful. They're just dreadful. You see?" He came to the end of the canvases and threw himself into a chair.

Eino walked silently around the room, looking at everything else, too. Finally he said, "You shouldn't mind so much about it. What you can be good at doesn't necessarily have to be in one particular vein."

"What could I do? I'm not good at anything."

"You're a good friend."

"How do you know?" Axel said thickly. "You hardly know me."

"I knew that the day we met. I always know who's going to be a friend. It's like knowing about women. Don't you?"

Axel belched and said that at the moment his luck with women was even more disastrous than his painting. "I spend most of my evenings staring at them through a pair of opera glasses. I can tell you the name of every girl in the *corps de ballet* just from her legs. But that's the nearest I get. Anyway, even before I came to Paris, somehow I never seemed to end up with the ones I really wanted. Except once, that time—and then I threw it away."

"That's all right," Eino told him. "I'll introduce you to some women."

Axel stood up. He reeled against the chair, fell back and tried to rest his elbow against the bookcase. He missed the first time. "That would be kind," he said.

*　　*　　*

He used to visit Karen's studio on his way back from work. Sometimes they'd go out together and sometimes they'd arrange to meet Eino for a meal. They all knew, without saying anything about it, that Marissa wouldn't want to join their party. And Axel had stopped wanting to see her.

He found that he could talk to Karen about art more easily than to Eino. She liked wandering through the museums with him. One day he spoke of a Scandinavian renaissance in the arts—painting, music, poetry: everything. And she said, "I suppose you got all that from Eino."

"No," he told her sharply, "I do have some ideas of my own."

She laughed, and said, "He's always talking about it, though. Isn't he?"

"He talks about all kinds of things."

"But mostly about how the Scandinavian countries are going to be a single cultural nation and at the moment they're like Italy before the unification."

"Oh, I wasn't thinking about all the political business."

"When we first met, he couldn't praise city life enough—especially Paris. Paris and the arts of Europe. But recently he's begun to change. I think it has something to do with his need to get away from Marissa. Now he says that we've got to go back to nature and back to the origins of Viking society. To study the trees and streams and mountains. Doesn't he? He's always talking about natural shapes and fundamental design."

"That's right. Why not? He's told me how to look for patterns everywhere. You wouldn't believe how many different shapes wind and water—"

"I detest nature," she said.

"How do you mean?"

"Crude, uncomfortable, formless, without a comprehensible style. Most women hate nature. I like civilized life, modern ideas. Eino wants to go backward. It's a kind of sentimentality. And the success of the venture would depend on a rebrutalizing of women—just as we've managed to bring things to the point where we're sometimes thought of as rational beings. What can one say to a man like that?"

"He reads a lot of Russian newspapers. They're always talking about—God knows what: German philosophy, that kind of thing."

"I don't take that seriously. I think he's much more interested in those English notions—he wants to build a model farm and have a school for weaving and furniture making, and do his own dyeing and make his own pots and vases and glassware. And silverware."

"He does talk about building a house."

"Precisely. My idea of a house is a little more like the governor's mansion than some pathetic old log cabin out in the pinewoods."

"He says it's got something to do with national identity."

"And what do you think?" she said suddenly. Her blue eyes looked back as if a trap had been sprung on him and she was watching from the outside. "Do you think," she asked, "that it's natural for a woman to live alone, without a husband or children?"

"No," he said. "I don't."

"Most people don't. But I love my life now. And I never used to be happy like this." She turned her head away and walked on, smiling. Axel wanted to know why she hadn't been happy before, but it was as if he'd been told not to ask. If he tried to find out, he was sure, she'd smile again and steer the talk another way.

Occasionally when he'd call to see Karen, she'd be out and the students would brew him a cup of tea or coffee. His favorite pupil in the school became the young German girl, Minna. He liked her work, too; it was strong, simple and noble, the subjects usually full-length nudes, often of children. She was also good at sculpting animals in clay.

He saw her sitting alone one day at a café table. He thought she might be waiting for a man, but he wanted to say hello anyway, so he stopped. She told him she wasn't waiting for anyone; she often sat at that table by herself because she liked the building across the street and it pleased her to see how the light fell over it as evening approached.

"But it's freezing," he said. "Let's go someplace warmer. You could catch pneumonia sitting here."

"Or something even more serious," she said. "Like what Karen's got."

He thought at first that she was making some sort of joke. Karen always had a beautiful, healthy glow in her cheeks and a sparkle in her eyes. Sometimes she'd cough a little—that was just a kind of habit, like the repeated use of a gesture.

"She's consumptive," Minna said.

"Impossible. She's the picture of health."

"The picture, maybe. Not the reality. She's very ill. It's gone so far that she won't see the doctors anymore. It's the reason why she left home. That's where she caught it."

"I can't believe it," he said.

She bowed her head sadly and looked back up. The building she liked had become part of the night while they'd been talking.

He took her to dinner. They discussed sculpture and Eino and her family back in Germany, who had all sworn they'd never speak to her again. Her mother had thrown a coffeepot after her the day she'd left.

She spoke of the integrity of form and the meaning of line, shape and color. "It's all action," she said.

A week later, he took her to bed. He told Eino, because Eino had introduced him to several women of easy ways and was constantly proposing to find him another. Now he didn't want any others. He didn't love Minna but he wanted to stay with her for a while. And he thought that she was in love with him; that made him happy.

"She's a nice girl," Eino said.

"And a very fine sculptress."

"Perhaps. And headstrong."

"Not at all," Axel said. "She's sweet and compliant. A loving, docile character."

"She walked right out on that family of hers, and they're a bunch of fire-eaters. That must have taken something. For a girl to leave home—"

"She had somewhere to go. She'd already written to Karen."

"Even so. If you leave home for good, these havens and shelters are always temporary. Staying with friends and studying at schools won't make up for it. She isn't the kind that should be on her own."

Axel suddenly had the feeling that Eino was trying to make him feel guilty. He didn't like it. He wasn't responsible for the girl. And it wasn't as if he'd been the first, although in fact that was something he hadn't considered until afterward.

"I'd ask you back," Eino told him, "but Marissa isn't very well."

"Because of the baby?"

"I suppose so. What's really doing it is that she whips herself into a frenzy of jealousy. Screaming and throwing things. I bang out of the house. Then I come back and she's screaming about where I've been, and then she cries for hours."

"I'm sorry."

"It's disgusting," Eino said. "I wish I were out of it. I'd walk out on her this minute if it weren't for Bruno. She's sent him to her aunt's."

"It'll be better when the baby's born," Axel said. "Give her something to think about."

"If it were anybody but Karen, it might make sense. I can't very well say she's the only one in town I haven't had."

"Minna tells me Karen's sick," Axel said. "Is it true?"

"She's got that cough."

"It isn't serious?"

"Of course not."

Axel was relieved. He believed it because he had come to believe whatever Eino told him.

Just as the snows cleared and the rains started, Karen summoned them both to her tea table. The painting and sculpting ladies had gone. They were alone in the apartment except for the cook and maid in the back rooms beyond the curtain. Karen took out a bottle and glasses. She poured three drinks, lifted her glass and said, "Minna's pregnant."

Axel drank a large gulp. He thought that Minna ought to have come to him first.

Karen said, "You've both been sleeping with her. Which one of you is going to marry her? She isn't a woman like Marissa, you know. That can't be allowed to happen."

Axel looked at Eino, who remained head down, staring at his drink.

"Another glass?" Karen asked.

Eino murmured, "I can't marry her. Not while Marissa is this way."

"Axel?" Karen said.

He took the second drink she was offering. He said that he'd have to talk to Minna herself before he could tell what he thought.

They were married in a rush. He wrote to his father and eventually received a letter back that expressed shock—which didn't worry him—and sadness, which upset him profoundly. The rest of the family wrote short, constrained letters. He felt that he'd been cut off from them forever. The cold rain beat on the windowpanes outside as he stood staring down into the street or across the way at the rooftops.

In the sixth month of her pregnancy, Marissa had a miscarriage. She nearly died. Eino stayed with her for a month afterward, to see that she recovered her health and to try to make her tell him where Bruno was. Then he left her. By that time Karen had begun to cough up blood: the doctors said it wouldn't be long.

She received callers without rising to her feet. On some days she looked normal, on others all at once she was gray as a corpse and it was as if the color had forsaken even her eyes. Axel came home one evening after seeing her and burst into tears. Minna put her hand on the back of his head. He was certain now, although she'd denied it, that the child she was carrying was Eino's and that Eino had been the one she'd loved all along; yet she was kind to Axel, as he was to her. He was fond of her. It wasn't what he wanted, but nothing ever was. Compared with the fact that Karen was dying, it didn't seem to matter, especially since he and Eino were such close friends.

Early in June Karen had a hemorrhage. She lived for four days after that. When Axel went to see her, she said, "Look at me now, Axel dear. This is nature." She smiled a terrible, delighted smile and whispered, "I'm not supposed to laugh. It starts me coughing again."

When her will was read, it turned out that she'd bequeathed a huge amount of money to found a combined school and artists' colony. It was all left in trust to Eino, who was to have sole power of decision over the disbursement.

"She must have loved you after all," Axel said.

"Don't be stupid," Eino told him. "She knew I could spend it in a way that would do some good. I was always telling her what I'd do if I had the chance. You'll help, won't you? You and Minna?"

"And Marissa?" Axel asked.

"Marissa sent me a letter as soon as she heard. Told me how glad she was that Karen had finally died; and said we could get married now, if I ever wanted to see my child again."

"Do you think she's insane?"

"No, only insufferable. She was always a bitch. It's just that a long time ago she used to be good in bed, too."

"She can't keep your child from you."

Eino answered that she'd already succeeded for months, but that he'd hired lawyers. That was as good as setting fire to your money, but there was no other solution. He'd get the boy and then go back to Finland. And as soon as Minna had the baby and was ready to move house, she and Axel ought to join them.

Axel said he'd contribute in any way he could. But when he was alone, he thought carefully about the scheme. He didn't believe it would be a good idea to ally himself so closely to a business enterprise that would depend on the friendship of a man who had no experience in business. He decided that after the birth of the child, he'd take Minna back to visit his family, and ask them for help.

*   *   *

During the long, light northern summers Axel used to work on the accounts early in the morning. At night he'd write poetry, which was even worse than his paintings had been back in Paris twenty years before. When the days grew shorter and colder and darker, he worked at night. He kept a bottle near his right hand. He'd pour out the drink systematically, so that there was always something in the glass. He sipped slowly and got through a couple of bottles a day. The alcohol never impaired his ability to count, though it had ruined his teeth, his circulation and his sleep. Nor had it inhibited the nimbleness of his mathematical juggling, the subtlety of his sense of proportion. When he falsified the figures in the books, it was all done in perfect ratio. That was why he was never going to get caught.

While he drank and wrote down the numbers, he'd cough a little, as he always did in the months of snow, but he hardly noticed that anymore. It seemed to be a part of the winter, or like a nervous tic that he'd lived with for half his life.

At one time he'd worked over the books with his cat, Bonaparte, sitting on his lap. Bonaparte was a dark, skinny animal, short-haired and soft. When Axel sat by the fire to read or just to daydream, Bonaparte would arrange himself with his paws around Axel's neck or with his nose pushed up into Axel's armpit. And Axel could think better: the cat's warmth and purring made him feel loved. But then, one summer, Bonaparte contracted the mange. Axel noticed that all at once his own hair was starting to fall out. And the children in the artists' colony caught ringworm.

The mothers in the community blamed the cat. That was nonsense, of course. It was much more likely that one of their odious brats had infected Bonaparte. After all, cats were very clean animals. Axel had probably said as much when he was drunk, although he didn't remember. There had been some kind of quarrel as the Philistines turned against him—that he did remember: using the name Philistine. And it was true; the wives and children and other relatives had nothing to do with art. They were living in the colony the way camp followers lived with an army—irrelevant to the war and often getting in the way.

A few days after the quarrel, he'd found Bonaparte outside on the doorstep, dead; he'd been torn to pieces. Maybe he'd been attacked by a wild animal, but it didn't seem possible that he'd be able to reach home with such injuries. Axel thought it more likely that one of the people he'd insulted had killed the cat out of spite and put him there, where Axel would find him in the morning.

And since then, he'd felt less guilty about the embezzlement. He should have had half the money, anyway. Karen had left it all to Eino because she'd thought that whatever kind of artistic movement they created out in the forests should be under the control of one person. She knew that Eino wouldn't be able to agree with anyone who had an opinion different from his own, whereas Axel could accommodate himself to other people's interests. Of course, she couldn't have known what was to happen to them.

From time to time Axel thought about her: her voice, her laughter, the way she'd looked in her green dress with the black velvet facings. He also thought that if he could dream up some way of doing it, he'd like to get back at Eino for having everything, while he had nothing. He'd had nothing since Paris and the scandal that had almost precisely coincided with his family's financial collapse—the landslide of bad luck that had swept them into bankruptcy, illness, emigration and death.

Eino's wife, Maria, worked on a hooked rug while she talked to him. She said, "He's always drunk. All the time, awake or asleep."

Eino made a small sound that didn't mean yes or no, but simply that he was listening. He moved his fingers along the side of a glass one of his students had made; the balance, the shape, everything was right. The young man had even invented his own design—a swirl of blue lay at the heart of the inner cup and appeared to swim in its white casing as the glass was turned.

"Isn't he ever going to leave?" she said. "I don't know why you put up with the man."

"Because we were young in Paris together," Eino answered, without taking his eyes off the glass. "He knew me when I was becoming what I am. He didn't become anything. He remained unfinished. Unexpressed." And when Karen's will was read out, Axel had been put in the position of a dependent.

"You aren't the one that has to feed him and wait on him," she complained, hitching the rug toward her.

"Is it such a hardship?"

"You aren't the one," she repeated.

"Don't be ungenerous." She wasn't normally so mean-minded against people. In her housekeeping she was thrifty —a good quality for a wife to have—but in her dealings with people she usually gave them some margin before deciding against them.

"And," she added, "I'm the one he tries to pester with his attentions."

Eino laughed. He couldn't imagine the moth-eaten, shambling Axel trying to win any favors from Maria, who had grown heroically buxom after the birth of her last child.

"And your daughter," she said. He didn't laugh at that. He turned in his chair to look at her, but she was staring down at her work. In a few minutes, she'd start up again. These conversations of hers could last for days. It took her a long time to drag all the evidence back and forth, to get to the stage where she could demand that he take action about something or other. Naturally he knew what she wanted this time. She wanted Axel to go.

He said, "He's useful to the community. I was never any good at bookkeeping and that kind of thing."

"And how good is he?"

"He was trained for it."

"I've sometimes thought he doctors the books."

"What does that mean?"

"Fiddling around with the figures, skimming some money off the top."

"It always balances out all right."

"Of course," she said. "That's how they do it."

Eino ran his eye over the row of glass objects on the shelf above his desk, at the chair to his right, the shawl hanging over the back of it, and the rug down on the floor. Everything he looked at had been made by craftsmen in the community—each article had its own unity and integrity. When one of his students finished a good piece of work, it was like a woman giving birth to a child she'd been forming inside her for months. Axel would never be able to know that kind of accomplishment. And he had no family, either.

"You have to make allowances for him," Eino said. "He's on his own and he's getting older."

"That just makes him harder to get along with."

"Please, Maria."

"It's true. He doesn't contribute. We could teach one of the young ones to handle the money."

"He's my friend," Eino told her. "I don't want to hear this." He turned back to the desk and picked up his magnifying glass. It probably wasn't really true that he and Axel were still friends, but they had been once. He thought: *Being a friend has destroyed Axel so that he hasn't lived his life. He's lived a small part of mine.*

They walked out into the woods by the path they'd taken long ago when they first visited the family on the other side of the lake. At that time the farmer, from whom Eino had bought the land, lived modestly on his homestead with his wife and three daughters and two sons. One of the daughters was pretty; she'd come in to pour water in the bathhouse. She'd had a shy smile and wore her hair in a long braid that hung down her back.

"I want to talk to you about something," Eino said.

There had been a fresh snowfall the night before. Everything was coated, white, still. The trees were like ranks of statuary around them. It was beautiful, but Axel's pleasure in the way it looked was accompanied by a sense of how dangerous it was. For several years he'd believed that when he died it would be the cold that would kill him.

"It's about the girls," Eino went on. "My own girls too, so it seems. They're too young for you, Axel. I don't blame you for wanting affection, but why don't you find yourself someone nearer your own age? A nice widow, something like that."

"I'm sick of leftovers," Axel said. His voice was harsh and the tone sour.

"I know it can't be easy out here, but a few weeks back in town, say, and you could meet somebody."

"Who would look at a man like me? You think I don't know what I've become?"

"A shave, some new clothes. Plenty of women would look at you."

"All the desperate ones. Some miserable old maid that looks like an elk in a corset."

"You'd have to sober up. It isn't too late for you to start off fresh, get married, have a family."

Axel smacked aside a branch full of snow. The bough sprang up, releasing a cloud of powdery crystals. He said, "I had a family once."

"That's over."

"Nothing's over till you die. I'm beginning to understand that. I've been having some dreams lately—you know, there was a long time when I didn't dream at all."

"Look at that," Eino said. He pointed to a place among the trees and rocks where one of the streams had melted and frozen again. The ice poured over itself in layers, its clear spaces mapped by ribs of depth and brightness: laced with white lanes, dark fissures, mines of shattered brilliance. "I'd like to make a vase like that. Just like that. And put spring flowers in it."

Axel looked. The place didn't seem very wonderful; just cold as hell, like everything else around him.

He used to think, back in Paris, how good it would be to breathe the fresh, cold air of his home. He'd stand by the windows and look out into the street, where the rain flooded down on the umbrellas of the crowds. Not even the rain could wash away the soot and grime. The air was no good. The rain itself came down dirty.

He thought that if they could get Karen to a better climate, she'd be all right. He tried to persuade her to go. She shook her head. Sometimes she was too tired to speak. Sometimes she'd actually refuse to see anybody. The school disbanded. Her servants were red-eyed when they opened the door to him. Eino said he'd tried to talk her into moving south and she'd told him that the doctors had already decided: it was too late for cures.

He met a student of hers in the museum one day: the old American woman, who started to sob, saying that it was too dreadful—a young life like that, and such a lovely girl; and when you thought of the real swine who were going to keep on eating and drinking for another forty years it almost made you despair. Yes, he agreed with her: there was no justice, no sense in it. He took her arm and walked through the galleries with her. She told him about how she'd fallen in love with paintings when she was a child; if she hadn't longed to paint, she'd have wanted to be an eye doctor, because vision—everything about its workings, even the fact that it was there at all—had always struck her as miraculous. "And now that I'm old," she ended, "I'm losing it, of course."

When he got back to the apartment, he told Minna about the meeting. She didn't appear very interested. She was reading a book on classical Greek sculpture. She kept turning over the pages of photographic plates. She said that everyone would miss Karen, naturally. He took up his post at the window again.

Karen died in the early summer. At the end she kept saying, "I can't breathe." Axel started to cough on the way to the funeral. As he left the cemetery grounds, he felt the cough coming on again. He disengaged himself from Minna, who was leaning on his right arm. "Handkerchief," he explained. He coughed, blew his nose and then raised his head and saw a woman turn the corner at the end of the street; she walked hurriedly and looked back. It was Marissa.

He told Eino. Eino said, "She never gives up." He'd left her, but she had the child, who was still down in the country

with one of her aunts, or an aunt's family. Several lawyers
had told him he didn't stand a chance of getting the boy back
through the courts. "If I knew where she was keeping him,
I'd just grab him."

"She could go to the police for that."

"I'd take him home. Right up north. He'd be fine there,
away from everything. It was the miscarriage that unhinged
her."

"She was always that way," Axel said, "only she used to
love you."

"I should have married Karen."

"You should have married Minna. Shouldn't you?"

"Don't you start. That's why I couldn't stand it anymore.
Marissa kept saying that Karen had stolen her baby before it
was born, and given it to Minna instead."

When people went crazy, Axel thought, what you saw was
usually simply the last stage of it, where everything broke.

He threw back a quick swallow of his drink and filled the
glass again, coughing as he'd been doing for nearly twenty
years. At first he'd believed he was imitating Karen. He'd
noticed before how for a time surviving friends and relatives
often mimicked the gestures or habits of speech they associ-
ated with someone dead. You could understand that—since
the missing person was on their minds—their unspoken
thoughts might announce themselves as movement. Minna
used to say that people thought with their whole bodies: if
you looked carefully, you could see it was true. But it might
be more than that. It might be that the mimicry was intended
somehow to keep the dead alive; that it was another repro-
ductive process: like art, like memory, like the imagination.

He hadn't forgotten Karen. While he drank, it was as if he
could remember talking to her just a few days before, being in
France: in Paris, in her drawing room with her. "And what
did you think of that hideous exhibition?" she'd say; or, "Tell
me about the bank, Axel. Who got what wrong today?"

His memory of her was much clearer than his recollection
of Minna. He recalled very little of the day when he came

home and found the police and the stretchers, and the caretaker in hysterics. It was as though most of that day had been burned from his life, the heat from it blurring and melting the time before and after. He just remembered that it seemed to be raining forever as the time drew near for Minna to give birth.

He knew, of course. But all the pictures that should have gone with the information had been erased. He must have had to look at Minna afterward, for instance, but he had no memory of it. He knew that Marissa, accompanied by Bruno, had climbed the stairs to the apartment. The caretaker had let them in. After that, most of the action could be pieced together only by what the caretaker was supposed to have heard. The police eventually came to the conclusion that Marissa, under the impression that Minna was carrying her lover's child, had entered the apartment, pulled out a pistol, shot the little boy, shot Minna, and then killed herself.

It took them a long while to figure all that out. In the beginning, they were only interested in Axel. They asked him suspiciously, accusingly: *Who is this woman named Marissa? Do you know her? If you don't know her, why did she kill your wife? Who is the child? Is the boy yours? How long have you known the woman? Did you love your wife? Did you quarrel with your wife? Was your wife a woman of easy morals, as some of these artistic people are? Did she leave a will?*

The questions were endless, coming down like the rain. He was ready to say anything to make them stop. He was prepared for them to take him out and put his head on the block. But Eino came and told them everything the right way around.

As he was drinking late at night he sometimes thought that it was curious: the catastrophe had made Eino stronger. It had even seemed to make him more intelligent; he'd come into focus after the killings. His speech, too, had changed. His talk was now incisive. When he spoke of the community's work, he cared about his subject and could make other people care, whereas before, he'd been a rough speaker, so bigoted that he could sound wholly ignorant. And, in contrast, the smooth speech of Axel's early years had grown rambling, disjointed, slurred.

He drank another glass. He finished the bottle. That night he had a dream.

He dreamt that he was standing at the entrance of a room that had a large table in it. Several people were seated around the table. There was talk and laughter, and an agreeable atmosphere of festivity. The host, at the end of the table, appeared delighted to see Axel and beckoned him in, greeting him warmly, and made him sit down next to him, where he had saved a chair. Axel felt extremely happy. His host then took up a decanter and poured out wine into a glass, which he handed to Axel. But Axel saw that the decanter had been emptied; he was the only one at the table who had any wine. He thought it would be rude to let the others go without anything. So he handed the glass back, in order that some of the wine could be given to the rest of the company. His host smiled, accepted the glass again, and, instead of doing what Axel had expected, turned to the sideboard nearby and set the glass there, where it remained throughout the course of the dinner.

There wasn't much more to the dream than that, but Axel was disturbed by it. He'd begun to feel out of place even when he was still in the dream. He'd obviously done something wrong while trying to be polite. The host hadn't exactly disapproved, but neither had he understood the reasoning behind the action of his guest.

In the morning Axel couldn't get up. One of the apprentices was sent over with some soup, but no one began to worry until the evening, when the doctor came—a young man whom Axel didn't trust or like.

"I'm all right," Axel told him. "No ringworm here."

"You're got a fever."

"It's the winter. I always do."

"Well, you shouldn't. Not like this."

Axel opened his mouth to argue, and an extraordinary thing happened: he leaned forward, gave a little cough, and was suddenly covered in blood. The doctor said, "God in heaven." Axel couldn't say anything; he was astounded at how easily it had happened, and almost without pain.

Eino came to see him. "You'll get well," he assured Axel. "We'll feed you up."

Axel stared morosely into Eino's face. He could get well, perhaps, but it was going to be a struggle if he had to put up with the horrible, healthy food they produced in the community—rough black bread and turnips, bean stew, cabbage forever. "A little beefsteak and champagne," he suggested, "might do me some good. It wouldn't hurt the rest of you, either. No wonder you're such a dreary bunch."

"Calm down, Axel. We'll get you better. I promise."

"Maybe. Yes, maybe. But you should have stayed in the cities, you know. Karen was right about that."

"We've talked that to death."

Axel laughed. He asked, "Where are you going to find spring flowers at this time of year?"

"What are you talking about?"

"Ice. I could go out into the snow right now and not feel it. I'm as hot as if I'd just come out of the sauna. We could go for a walk."

"Tomorrow, maybe."

"I don't know why you think I'd be interested in your wife. I wouldn't want her even for a holiday weekend. Hunched over her nasty handwoven things, nagging—"

"That's enough, Axel."

"Anyway, I've got a wife of my own. Wonderful girl, full of character. Beautiful black hair. Fine artist. She was so good to me. I know she never loved me, but she was really nice to me. You can't imagine."

Eino pushed his chair back and rushed out of the cabin. He returned in the morning to see if Axel was better, but the fever continued.

Axel lay in his bed and thought. He sweated and drowsed and wondered how he could pay Eino back for not helping him. Eino had everything, and now he thought he was such a great hero, too. He was busy changing the world. Finnish art and culture wasn't enough for him—on top of all that, he wanted to change Finnish politics. *Finland for the Finns*, he'd say: *Our art must be our own, from our own forms—rivers, stones, trees—and our ideas should be our own as well, not Swedish or Russian or German.*

It didn't make sense to bury yourself in the country if you wanted to do anything higher than farming. Art flourished among the bright lights. Down in the country all you could raise was beets and manure. *Man is a city-dwelling animal:* Alex remembered that from school. "City-dwelling" was usually translated as "political." And Eino was just as wrong about that; to go forward, they needed to copy and import more ideas—to become international. A lot of small countries had become great because they'd gone out and brought the rest of the world back to their people, not closed the doors against outside influence.

Eino was wrong. On the other hand, Eino had succeeded. He hadn't lost heart because the French were always going to be better painters. He'd just gone ahead and done the work he'd planned for himself. And it was good, you had to give him credit for that; and not like anybody else's, either. Nevertheless, it wasn't art. It was tables and chairs. And furthermore—why was it that Eino, always so desirable to women, invariably settled down with the ugly ones? He'd never built that big house he'd wanted, either.

Axel dozed and woke again. The fire was high: someone must have come in and built it up while he'd slept, and gone away again. There was a soup tureen on the table beside him, a bowl of fruit, and buttered bread on a plate. He wasn't hungry. He turned away from them.

He remembered his family, the houses where he used to live; he thought about his parents: as they were when he left home to go to Paris, and before that, in his childhood. They'd given him plenty of good advice and help. Had he wanted to end like this?

Why had he been so obsessed by the idea of becoming an artist? If he'd decided just to have a good time instead, he could have been happy. Maybe there was something in him, like a weight, that would always drag him down. He knew that—probably—if he had kept his mouth shut all those years ago, he could have held on to the girl in St. Petersburg, made several rich friends, gone to many splended dinners and balls and other celebrations: become known and liked by a crowd of interesting people, and—possibly—have won her in the end, although that wasn't likely: there had been other, more sophisticated young men around, and also less sophisticated, if she'd had a mind to try that too. Of course, she might have forced him into the stand he'd taken. She might have wanted an excuse to break with him. The attitude of the maid had suggested that. Not that any of it mattered. In any case, he had lost. But most of the loss was his fault. He should have caught hold of whatever he could get, and enjoyed it.

He remembered his dream about the host who had offered him the glass of wine. And suddenly he realized the meaning of it: the host was God and he had given Axel the full glass he was meant to drink. It couldn't be distributed among any of the other guests because it was intended for him alone. It had been the life he was supposed to live. And when he had refused it, it had to go unused by anyone.

He wanted to cry out with anger and grief. He'd missed the whole of his life. And he knew that—as he had once hoped—his life had indeed been picked out, from the beginning, to be the life of an artist, which wasn't like the life of other men. An artist's life was his work. He thought: *How disappointed God must be in me. How disappointed I am in myself.* He hadn't believed in God for years.

He knew what he should do: he should get out and go to the south—the real south, where he'd be able to recover his health. But he couldn't now. He'd left it too late.

After two days, he thought he was better. He wanted to get up. Eino came to visit him and sat by the bed; he told Axel the doctor had said he was to stay indoors, although if he wanted to move to the writing table or the sofa, that would be all right. Axel got up out of bed and fainted.

When he came to again, he was sure he was near death. "You'll get well," Eino told him.

"Of course I won't. I'm going to die. You're the one who's

going to live. And you deserve to, because you didn't refuse the glass. I should have known how important it was."

Eino looked around him. He shot a glance toward the foot of the bed, at the side, where Axel used to stash his empty bottles. "What glass?" he said.

Axel pretended to sleep. A picture came to him, like a dream, of Maria sitting by the fire and working on a piece of material. He thought it was sure to be one of her hooked rugs, but when he looked more closely he saw with horror that it was a long, gray chain of little people that she was knitting. She was producing the future. Then he was staring at the wall and realizing that he'd fallen asleep after all.

He'd been right in the first place to distrust the idea of living in one of these artists' colonies. He ought to be near the bustle and variety of a modern city, not buried in some fantasy of Eden, where the food had no real taste and the people were all the same. The women, the girls, were like the lumpy food: standing there with their mouths open while you tried out a little persiflage—nothing too complicated, no elaborate scrollwork or classical vocabulary—and then giggling or laughing loudly. Their laughter was like the quacking of ducks, the braying of donkeys. It took an effort to believe that they were human. He used to be accustomed to good society—not at the top, but men and women who could hold a conversation. Even Eino wasn't up to that. He'd thought Eino was some sort of rough-hewn genius, but actually he was only an obstinate craftsman with a love of the peasant traditions.

Suddenly it infuriated him that not only was he going to miss being an artist and living an interesting life, but he'd tied himself to someone else who was, in his own way, second-best. It was like being a wife who finds out twenty years too late that she's chosen the wrong man.

"He's starting to go a little crazy," Eino said.

"He was always like that," Maria told him. "Even before he started to drink so much."

"This is different. I suppose it's the illness."

"What does the doctor say?"

"As much as he knows, and that isn't much."

"I think," Maria said, "there are some artists who go off their heads. And there are other people who go crazy because they aren't artists. That's Axel. He doesn't have any talents, not for anything."

"He's got a talent for friendship."

"Oh?" she said. "Are you sure?"

"Let's leave all this," Eino said, "till we know when he's going to get better." He went to visit Axel again. He was astonished by the change in him.

Axel was sitting up in the chair. He was fully clothed and wearing his heavy outdoor boots. His coat, scarf and hat were on the table next to him. His face looked deathly. He said, "I was waiting for you, Eino. I wanted to take one last walk with you."

"I don't think you should, Axel."

"I need to. If I can't get all the way back, you can bring me home. Or you can leave me."

"I don't think the doctor would like it."

"You know that doctor—that doctor only likes healthy people. He can't do anything for me. You're the one who can help. You can take me for a walk." He stood up and reached out quickly to touch the table.

Eino thought they probably wouldn't make it past the two neighboring cabins. He said all right.

They started off down the path that led into the woods. The sun was out. There was no wind, but it was a day of intense, dry cold. Axel started to talk.

"I remember going through the museums in Paris with you," he said. "I was fascinated by the things you told me; your whole life. One day you said you'd been living on pumpernickel sandwiches recently and that meant two slices of bread with a piece of pumpernickel between them. I was so shocked by everything and so pleased. You took me to meet the Italian who used to be a glassblower and you ran your fingers down the outside of a vase and said you could tell the lead content that way. I couldn't believe it. Then you laughed and said: it was like everything else, you had to have a feeling for it. You said that the forests of Finland were better than the finest museums and I believed you. I came here. I remember that girl, the farmer's daughter; when she bent down to pour out the water; her shoulders and back. I thought maybe humanity was still possible for me. But you told me you'd always been interested in glass more than anything else, because it was the medium closest to ice. Eino, the first winter we were here, I had my warning. I was walking along this very trail, right about here—and something fell from above, just in front of me: plop! and there it was—a bird. It had died in the air. It must have been lost too, at that time of the year. I'd heard such a thing was possible, but to have it happen to me, after everything else—no. This beauty and nobility of nature you'd been telling me about; I thought it was all lies. It seemed to me that nature was pitiless: it was engaged in a constant effort to annihilate what was already there, in order to produce new forms. Or to come up with one more form just like the last one. It was only interested in moving onward. I began to understand the character of Judas. I knew that he must have been a man who watched his friend with sympathy until the moment when he realized that the friend was wrong and stupid, and that none of his ideas would work, and shouldn't be allowed to, anyway."

"Stop talking, Axel," Eino said.

"How dark it is in the winter, all the time. The snow. Of course the snow has its own brightness, but the light goes out of the sky. It isn't fair. The cold goes on too long. It makes me feel horrible sometimes."

"You'll feel better in the spring."

"How am I going to feel better? I've got what Karen had."

"The doctors are learning new things every minute. Someday people won't have these diseases."

"But what makes anyone catch diseases? Some do and some don't. That's heredity. Or is it? Nobody understands that, either. What do we know at all? What have we ever learned?"

"Well," Eino suggested, "there's photography. That's quite an extraordinary thing, isn't it? Much more complicated than most machines."

"Yes," Axel said, calmed. "Yes, that's right. That was a great discovery."

"And there are the arts."

"Oh, that was the one thing I could always understand. I just couldn't do it, that's all. And I don't know anymore why people try to do anything in life. None of it has any meaning without beauty, and beauty goes—it just evaporates. Look, like snow. Like youth, Eino. Like all of us, everything. What was it for?"

"For the ones who come after us."

"The hell with them. It's going to be the same for them as it's been for us."

"No, it's going to be better. We'll leave them that inheritance."

"That's idiotic. One good war can wipe out what ten generations create. In times of need, everything goes by the board. If life gets hard enough, people eat anything. They'd eat the paint off the Sistine Chapel. They'd eat the face off the Botticelli Venus."

"Stop talking so much," Eino said. "You're tiring yourself out. I think we should go back."

Axel stopped. They had come almost to the end of a plantation where the regularly spaced trees were so encrusted and massy with snow that they no longer resembled living, growing things; they looked like structures built for some purpose, as if to guard a fortress or line the approach to a palace that wasn't there. Now that the day was giving out, a bluish light seemed to come from all the weight of ice on them.

Axel took a few more steps forward. Beyond the trees lay a long, open stretch of land that was absolutely even and blank. "You want me to leave," he said. "All right, I'm leaving."

"It's too cold to stay out here, Axel. Come on."

"Look, Eino."

"If you don't come now, I'm going to knock you out and carry you back."

"Look. Don't you see?" Axel stumbled forward. A gigantic, bursting whiteness flowered everywhere around him, over the entire country, over the world: a white like the blossoming of trees in the spring. Everything else gave way to it, even the thought of color. He would have laughed, if it hadn't been so cold. It was cold enough to snatch the breath from your body and keep it.

"You were always pointing things out to me," he said, "and I never saw: forms, shapes, patterns. I thought I knew what you were talking about. But now I'm seeing them, Eino. Look, there in the snow—it's the wing of a dove. Perfect. And over there another one, like a fan of feathers, and next to it all the white flowers. And this house around us: the house—don't you see?"

Eino followed, keeping his hands ready in case Axel started to fall. They walked far out into the open: into an immense, white-filled space that was flat and silent. "No," he said, "I can't see anything."

"But it's everywhere. I'm seeing them, Eino. I'm seeing everything. God, what a feeling. Like a sword going into me. All this beauty."

"Axel, we've got to get you back to the house."

Axel stood away and faced Eino. He coughed a little.

"We can talk about this later," Eino said.

"Wonderful forms," Axel whispered. "Beautiful shapes." He began to wave his arms, lost his balance and toppled straight backward onto the ground, where he lay motionless, arms and legs outspread. His eyes, as still as ice, looked toward the sky.

IN THE ACT

As long as Helen was attending her adult education classes twice a week, everything worked out fine: Edgar could have a completely quiet house for his work, or his thinking, or whatever it was. But when the lease on the school's building ran out, all the courses would end—the flower arranging, the intermediate French and beginning Italian, the judo, oil painting and transcendental meditation.

She told Edgar well in advance. He nodded. She repeated the information, just in case. He said, "Mm." Over the next two weeks she mentioned the school closure at least three times. And, after she and her classmates had had their farewell party, she told him all about that, adding, "So, I'll be at home next week. And the week after that. And so on."

"Home?" Edgar said. "What about your adult education things?"

She went over the whole history one more time. At last he was listening. He looked straight at her and said, "Oh. That means you'll have to find something else to occupy yourself with on those afternoons."

"I suppose so. I might stay home and paint here."

"I'll be busy up in the lab."

"I could make a kind of studio down in the cellar."

"I'll be working. I need absolute peace and quiet."

"Well, painting isn't very loud."

"Helen," he said, "I'd like to have the house to myself."

She never got angry with him anymore; that is, she'd discovered that it did no good: he'd just look at her coldly as if she were exhibiting distressing habits usually encountered only among the lower species. Raising her voice—when she'd been driven to it—produced the same reaction from him. She'd learned to be argumentative in a fudgy, forgiving drone she'd found effective with the children: enough of that sound and the boredom level rose to a point where people would agree to anything. Edgar had a matching special tone for private quarrels: knowing, didactic, often sarcastic or hectoring. Whenever he used it outside the house, it made him disliked. It was a good voice for winning arguments by making other people hysterical. His hearing seemed to block off when it started.

She said, "If you'd like the house to yourself, you can have it. Maybe you wouldn't mind fixing some supper for us while you're here. That way, I'd have something to look forward to, soon as I get in from walking around the block five thousand times."

"There's no need for that."

"OK, you can take me out. Twice a week. That'll be nice. We could see a lot of new movies in just a month."

"You're being unreasonable."

"Of course I am. I'm a woman," she said. "You've already explained that to me."

"Let's not get into that."

"Why not? If I'm not even allowed to paint downstairs somewhere for two afternoons a week? I never come up to the attic, do I?"

"You're always tapping on the door, asking me if I want a cup of coffee."

"Only that once."

"It was a crucial moment."

"Well, now you've got your thermos bottle and everything, you're all set up there."

"You came up other times."

"That big noise—explosion, whatever it was: of course I did. I was worried. You could burn the house down."

"I think this is time number fourteen for telling you that the experiments are not dangerous."

"Fourteen? I'm sure that must be right. You keep track of things like that so well. Each time I conceived, it was a positive miracle of timing. I can remember you crossing off the days on the calendar."

"You're trying to sidetrack me."

"I'm trying to get you to allow me to stay in my own house."

"I really do need complete freedom to work. It simply isn't the same when somebody else is in the house. Even if you didn't try to interrupt me again."

"The only other time I knocked on the door was when there was all the screaming."

"I told you," Edgar said. "I got the volume too high."

"It sounded like real people."

"It was a tape."

"For heaven's sake, Edgar—where can I go?"

"See some friends? Look around a museum or two. Find another one of those adult education places."

All at once she felt hurt. She didn't want to argue anymore, even if there was a hope of winning. She was ready to walk out and tramp up and down the streets like a child running away. She said, "I'll try," and went into the living room. She walked around the corner, into the alcove where the desk was. She sat down in the plump, floral-patterned chair, put her knees up and curled into a ball. She heard his feet going up the stairs, then up the next flight to the attic. He wouldn't be wondering whether he'd made her miserable. He'd be getting out the keys to unlock the attic door, which he kept locked all the time, and if he was inside, bolted too. He'd be sighing with pleasure at the prospect of getting back to his experiment. Of course he was right: she'd have to find something to do with her time. But just for a few minutes, she'd stay in the flowered chair, with her arm over her eyes.

The next morning, she was angry. He read through his newspaper conscientiously, withdrawing his attention from it for only a few seconds to tell her that she hadn't cut all the segments entirely free in his grapefruit—he'd hit exactly four that were still attached. She knew, he said, how that kind of thing annoyed him.

She read her letters. Her two sons were at boarding school. Edgar approved. She herself would never have suggested sending, or allowing, the boys to go away: in fact, the suggestion had come from them. They had suddenly clamored for the expensive snobberies of the East Coast; they needed, they wanted, they couldn't live without education at the last of the all-male establishments. Helen's attendance at adult education classes dated from the time of their emigration.

Both of the boys had written to her. Usually she was delighted by whatever they had to say. This morning their news seemed to be nothing but boastful accounts of how they had won some sports event or beaten another boy at something, shown him who was who; and so forth. She was probably lucky they were far away. That would have been two more grapefruits she wouldn't be able to get right.

When she passed the letters over to Edgar, he was soberly pleased with the boys' victories. He wasn't too bad as a father. He wasn't actually too bad anyway, except that sometimes he irritated her to distraction. She still couldn't believe he was asking her to get out of the house every Tuesday and Thursday, so he'd have the whole place to himself.

"What's wrong with the coffeepot?" he added.

She snapped back out of her thoughts. "I was wondering about adult education classes," she told him.

"Fine. More of that flower arranging, or maybe a new language."

"Yes, maybe. Who would I talk to in a new language?"

"Well, the teacher. Anybody else who speaks it." He went back to the paper. Soon afterward he took his last sip of coffee, looked around for his briefcase, and left the house for the pathology laboratories where he had his job. They did a lot of work for the police as well as for hospitals and private clinics. His specialty was hemoglobin.

With the dusting and vacuuming she worked off some of her vexation. Then she sat down with a cup of coffee. She phoned about the plumber's bill, the bracelet link that was supposed to be done but still wasn't, the garage. Nothing was ready. She was about to call up her friend, Gina, to complain about life in general, when she had a better idea: she'd go up to the attic.

She had a key. Long before the day when there was the explosion or the one when she'd heard the screams, she had wanted to see inside his laboratory. The loud noise had at first scared her off from the idea of trespassing, and then reinforced her initial desire: to go in and take a look around— make sure everything was all right up there. The screams too, at first frightening, had made her eager to see, to know; for a few moments she had been convinced that there were real people up there. Not that Edgar would be carrying out any experiment that would cause pain to someone, but—she didn't really know what she thought about it all.

The way he locked the door before he came downstairs; the way he locked up as soon as he entered the lab and shut the door behind him, shooting the bolt across: it made her nervous. If there was nothing inside that could harm her, it was an insult to keep her out. On the other hand, if there was something dangerous up there, did she dare go in and find out about it?

The key was one of the extras from the Mexican bowl that had been shoved over to the end of a workbench in the cellar. The bowl was filled with old keys. Helen had looked through the whole collection when they had moved in; she'd assumed that they came from other houses or even from workplaces long vanished. There were about fifty keys, some large, long and rusted, like the sort of thing that might be needed for a garden gate or a toolshed. After the screams, when her frustration and curiosity about the lab had reached a sudden peak, she'd remembered the bowl of keys. Some could be discounted straightaway, but about a dozen were possible.

The one that fitted was an ordinary brass key. She'd unlocked the door, pushed it open slowly, peeked in and locked up again. She hadn't stepped over the threshold. Now, standing in the middle of her living room rug, she wondered why she hadn't gone in and had a thorough look at everything. She seemed to recall that what was in the room had been fairly uninteresting: tables, benches, racks of test tubes, a microscope, a couple of Bunsen burners, two sinks, a bookcase against the wall. Never mind: this time she'd go through the place carefully.

She got the key and started up the stairs, moving fast. She had the door open before there was time to think about it. The room looked slightly different from when she'd last seen it, and more crowded. There were more bottles, jars and test tubes. Standing racks had been added at the far end, where the empty steamer trunks used to be. She also remembered a rather nice sofa; more a like a *chaise longue*. Edgar had occasionally stayed up in the lab overnight, working while she'd watched the late movie downstairs, or read a detective story. She'd always thought the sofa was too good to leave up in the attic, but Edgar had insisted that he needed it. Now she couldn't see it. But, as she moved forward, she noticed with surprise that a bathtub had been added to the collection of sinks and troughs; it was an old, high-standing type. She couldn't imagine how Edgar had managed to get it in there. He'd have had to hire people. *Out of the van and to the front door*, she was thinking; *up the stairs*. She began to worry about the weight. Even though the house was well built and strong, and most of the heavy equipment stood around the sides, it wasn't a good idea to fill up a place with too many heavy objects. Edgar had undoubtedly gone into the question of beam stress and calculated the risks; he'd have found out all about the subject. Of course, every once in a while, he was wrong.

She looked into the first alcove: empty. She turned into the second, bigger one. There was the sofa. And there was a bundle of something thrown on top of it, wrapped in a sheet. She was about to pass by when she saw a hand protruding from one of the bottom folds of the sheet.

She let out a gurgled little shriek that scared her. She looked away and then back again. Propped against the edge of the sofa's armrest was a leg, from the knee down. Next to it lay an open shoe box containing fingers. She began to feel that her breathing wasn't right. She wanted to get out, but there was still the question of what was under the sheet. She had to know that. If she ran out without looking, she'd never summon the courage to use the key again.

She counted to ten, wiped her hands down the sides of her skirt and told herself that whatever the thing was, it couldn't be worse than what they were liable to show you nowadays on television, even in the news programs. She reached out and pulled down the edge of the sheet.

It was pretty bad: a head with the face laid bare. The muscles, tendons and other bits across the face were mainly red or pink, a few of them darker than she'd imagined things like that were supposed to be. But they weren't wet; there was no blood. She bent her knees and looked more closely. From inside the still open skull she caught the glint of metal. There were lots of small wheels and bolts and tubes inside, like the interior of a watch or a radio.

She straightened up, rearranged the sheet and gently put out a hand toward the half leg. She felt the skin below the place where the joint should have been attached to some knuckly part of a knee.

A chill ran over her scalp. The skin, though unwarmed, was creamy, smooth, soft and silky, uncannily delicious to the touch. She pulled back her hand. For about five minutes she stood just staring at the wall. Then, she understood. The body wasn't real. Naturally, it couldn't be real: a dead body would have to be refrigerated. Therefore, that thing there on the sofa in pieces was not a corpse Edgar had taken from the pathology morgue; it was a body he had built himself out of other materials. Why on earth he'd want to do such a thing was beyond her.

She left everything in place, closed the door behind her and locked it with her key. Later in the day the answer came to her: her husband must be pioneering research on victims of road accidents. She had read an article several years before, about a medical school that simulated injuries by strapping life-sized replicas of people into cars; after smashing them up, they studied the damaged parts. The project had been funded by an insurance company. No doubt Edgar was working on something similar, although greatly in advance of anything she'd heard about. That skin, for example, was fantastic. And all the intricate bands of muscle and everything—the thing was very complicated. She still didn't understand what the clockwork mechanism in the head would be for, but maybe that would have something to do with a remote-control guidance system. The whole business was explainable. She stopped feeling scared. Nevertheless, she was thankful that the eyelids had been closed.

Edgar worked hard up in the attic for several days. She thought she'd give him a week and then go up and check on the progress he'd made. In the meantime, she looked into the possibilities of new adult education schools. She had lunch with Gina, who was worried about her daughter's weight problem and who poured out a long story to her about psychologists, behaviorists, weight-watchers and doctors. Helen listened sympathetically; she was glad to have such a convoluted narrative to concentrate on—there was no room for temptation to talk about what was troubling her: Edgar and the activity he was engaged in up in the attic.

Two days later, Mr. Murdock from the old oil painting classes asked her to tea with Pat and Babs. The three of them cheered her up. Mr. Murdock had already left the new classes they'd joined; the other two were going to, but for the moment they were sticking it out in order to be able to report back all the latest stories about the odious Miss Bindale. Miss Bindale was driving everyone away; she might end by causing the teacher to resign, too. It was a shame, they all said: one person could spoil everything. Mr. Murdock recommended a language school he'd gone to for French. The place wasn't so much fun as their adult education school—it was more serious, the classes were mostly for businessmen and unless you applied for the weekend, everything was in the evening. Pat said, "It'd be a really good way to meet men. If you don't want the address, I'll keep it myself."

"You'll never get anywhere if it's a language," Babs told her. "Car maintenance, that's the one. There aren't any other women at all."

"Or karate," Helen said.

"I wouldn't try it. You pick the wrong type there—they'll throw you against the wall and say it was an accident because they forgot to leave out some basic move. No thanks."

Pat said that a friend of hers, named Shirley, had gone to a couple of other adult education places and had given her the addresses; four different ones. "I liked the first one, so I never tried the others, but I can send you the addresses. I'll take a good look around, see where I put that piece of paper."

Edgar spent the whole of the weekend up in the lab:

Saturday night and Sunday too. He came down for meals. On Friday he'd brought her flowers, given her a talk about why the work was going to be necessary; when, where and how he'd expect his meals during the period; and how he appreciated her cooperation. She said, "Yes, dear," to everything, put his red roses in a vase, took it into the living room and told him they looked lovely. She preferred daffodils, chrysanthemums, tulips, daisies, stock, sweet peas, asters: almost anything. And if they had to be roses, any color other than red.

He stayed in the bedroom Friday night, making sure that she didn't feel neglected. He wanted her to be satisfied with the arrangements. She was not only satisfied; she was surprised.

She carried out her appointed cooking tasks with grim cheerfulness. She could hardly wait until Monday, when he'd be out of the house and she could go look at what he'd been doing.

On Sunday she knew that he'd achieved some kind of breakthrough in the work. He was transformed, radiant. He looked tired, but serene. Whatever it was, was finished. However, he didn't say anything about coming downstairs. He stayed up in the attic that night.

The next morning she waited awhile after he'd gone. She was going to give him enough time to get all the way to work, and more: in case he'd forgotten something and had to come back for it. She wanted to be able to look at everything and not feel rushed. Whatever he'd completed was still up in the attic—all he'd taken with him was his briefcase.

She did the dishes, made the bed, checked her watch. She looked out of the window, although she didn't need to: it was one of those unnecessary things people do when they're anxious about something. She got the key.

The attic workroom looked the same, as far as she could see. She stepped in, closing the door lightly, so that it touched the jamb but didn't click into the frame. She walked forward. Her eyes jumped from place to place.

She peered into the first alcove: nothing. She hurried to the second; there was the sofa. And on it lay a young and beautiful woman: the creamy skin was as it had been before. The face had been fitted with its outer coating; everything there was in place: the lilac-tinted eyelids with long, dark lashes, the cupid's-bow mouth, the small, pert nose.

The face lay in the center of a cloudlike nest of twirly blond ringlets. A blue ribbon peeped out from a bunch of them at the back. The dress she wore was pink and cut like some sort of ballerina costume: the bodice like a bathing suit top, the skirt standing out with layers of net and lace and stiffening. Her feet and legs were bare. The toenails, like the nails on the fingers, had been painted red.

Helen reached out toward the left leg. She ran her hand over it, stopped, and then quickly pulled back. The skin was warm. She moved along the side of the sofa, to where she could be near the head. "Wake up," she ordered. There was no response. Naturally: this wasn't a person—it was some kind of doll. It was so lifelike that it was almost impossible to believe that; nevertheless, her husband had built it.

As she stood there, trying to imagine why Edgar should have made a doll so detailed in that particular way, with painted nails and a blue satin bow and everything, she began to wonder how lifelike the rest of the body was. That was an important question.

If she hadn't seen the thing in its partly assembled state the week before, she wouldn't have known this was a replica, a machine. But having seen it complete, there was—all at once—no doubt in her mind that her husband had invented it for his own private purposes: otherwise, why make it so definitely nonutilitarian?

She thought she'd better know what she was up against. She examined the doll thoroughly, taking off the pink dress first, and then the black lace bra and underpants. She started to lose her sense of danger. She was getting mad. Who else, other than Edgar himself, could have chosen the pink dress and black underwear? He couldn't walk into a dress shop in her company without becoming flustered, yet she could picture him standing at a counter somewhere and asking for the clothes, saying in his argument-winning voice, "Black lace, please, with a ribbon right about here." He'd known the right size, too—but of course he'd known that. The doll had been built to specification: his specifications. *Oh*, Helen thought, *the swine*.

And the thing was so real-looking. She was sitting on the edge of the sofa and fiddling around with the doll's head, investigating the way the hair grew, when she felt her finger push down on what must have been a button behind the left ear.

The doll's eyelids rose, revealing a pair of enormous blue eyes. The lips parted in a dazzling smile, the torso began to breathe.

"Oh," Helen said. "Oh dear."

"Oh dear," the doll repeatedly gently. "What can the matter be?"

Helen thought she might be going crazy. She asked—automatically and politely—"Who are you?"

"I'm fine," the doll told her. "How are you?"

"Not how. Who?"

The doll smiled lovingly and relapsed into an expression of joyful delight. The eyelids blinked every once in a while. Helen watched. The action had evidently been programmed to be slightly irregular, to avoid an impression of the mechanical. Still, there was something hypnotic about it. The lips were silent. The voice too must be on a computer: the doll would only answer if you spoke to it. The voice-tape scanner didn't seem to be quite perfect yet, either.

She was trying to push the button again, to turn off the eyelids, when she hit a nearby second button instead and sent the machine into overdrive. The lids drooped, the arms went up and out, the knees flew apart, the hips began to gyrate in an unmistakable manner, and the lips spoke.

Helen shot to her feet, stumbled back a few steps and crashed against the wall. She folded her arms and stayed where she was, staring with memorizing intensity while the doll went through the cycle it had begun. Probably there were many other things it could do—this would be merely one of the variations. Out of the rosebud mouth came a mixture of baby talk and obscenity, of crude slang and sentimentality.

She gripped the sides of her arms and waited sternly until the exercise appeared to be over, though the doll was still begging in sweetly tremulous whispers for more. She stepped forward and slapped it across the face. "Darling," it murmured. She scrabbled among the golden curls, grabbed the ear and pushed every button she could see. There were five, all very small. They looked like pinheads. There were also two tiny switches she decided to leave alone. She'd seen enough. She was quivering with rage, shame and the need for revenge.

When she thought about wearing herself out doing the shopping and cooking and scrubbing, she prickled all over with a sense of grievance. She'd been slaving away for years, just so he could run up to the attic every evening and keep his secrets. And the boys were turning into the same kind as their father: what they wanted too was someone menial to provide services for them. And then they could spend their lives playing.

She saw herself as a lone, victimized woman beleaguered by selfish men. Her anger gave her a courage she wouldn't otherwise have had.

She ran out and across the hall to the other side of the attic—the side that wasn't locked. There were the trunks and suitcases, including the nice big one with wheels. There too was the chest full of spare blankets and quilts. She pulled out two of the blankets and took them into the lab. Then she carried the suitcase downstairs to the front hall.

She went up to the attic again, dressed the doll in its clothes, rolled it into the blankets and dragged them across the floor and down the stairs. She unzipped the suitcase, dumped the doll inside, folded the legs and arms and began to pack it tight, zipping the outside as she stuffed the pink skirt away.

She went up to the attic one more time, to put the blankets back and to shut the door of the lab.

She got her coat and handbag. The suitcase was easy to manage until she had to lift it into the back of the car. That wasn't so easy. Edgar was the one with the big car. Still, she could do it. All she'd have to worry about would be steps.

The doll seemed to weigh exactly the same as a real woman of equivalent height and size.

There were three choices: the airport, the bus depot and the train station. The train station was large and nearer than the airport. She'd try it first.

Everything went well. She found a parking space straight-away and was able to wheel the suitcase across the road, onto the sidewalk and through the doors, up an escalator and across several waiting rooms, to the locker halls. There was a whole bank of extra-large lockers; she heaved the case into one of them, put in enough money to release the key, and went to get some more coins. She ended up having to buy a paperback book, but the woman at the cash register agreed to let her have two big handfuls of change. She fed the money meticulously into the slot. The suitcase would be paid up for over two weeks.

Ron was getting out of his car when he saw the woman slam her car door and start to wheel the suitcase across the parking lot. She looked possible: the case seemed heavy.

He followed, walked casually. He had a repertoire of walks calculated to throw off suspicion. He hadn't had to learn any of them—they came naturally, like all his other athletic talents. That was what he was always telling Sid down at the gym: *I got natural talent. I don't need nobody teaching me nothing.* He still couldn't understand how Sid had knocked him out in the third round. He hadn't given up the idea that something had been slipped into his Coke. Sometimes there was a lot of heavy betting going on, even when you were just sparring.

She looked like a nice, respectable woman; pretty, took care of herself. The kind that said no. Her clothes cost something, which was a good sign; so was the trouble she had getting the wheels of the case up onto the curb. Of course, she could be getting on a train.

He followed her all the way around the corner to the lockers. He watched, standing against the wall and pretend-ing to look at his paper. When she was through, he followed her far enough to see that she was coming back. She put a lot of money in the locker: good—the case would be there a while. But he'd probably better get it quick, before somebody else did.

She left the building. That might mean she was going for a second suitcase that she hadn't been able to handle in the same load. He looked around, folded his paper, held it to cover what he was doing, and stepped up to the locker. He took a metal slide out of his pocket and stuck it into the keyhole. It was a cinch.

Some people could never have looked unsuspicious while wheeling away stolen luggage, but you had to believe in yourself: that was the main thing. Ron did his best. He didn't hurry. He got the bag into the backseat of his car and started off. Her car, he noticed, was already gone.

Normally he'd have stopped just around the block somewhere, to go through the contents; but the traffic was building up. He decided to drive straight on home. He was beginning to get curious about what was inside. The suitcase was really heavy. The moment he'd pulled it from the locker he'd thought: *Great—gold bars; silver candlesticks.* A lot of people had those lockers. She hadn't looked like that type, but how could you ever tell? She could be helping a pal, or a husband. A guy he knew had found some cash once—a whole overnight bag full of the stuff. And all of it counterfeit, it turned out; he'd done time for that.

He got the bag out of the car, into the apartment block where he lived, up three floors in the elevator, down the hall to his bedroom. He broke the locks as soon as he'd thrown his jacket over the back of the easy chair. He unzipped both sides.

A powerful odor of mothballs was released into the room as the lid sprang open, disclosing a blond woman in a pink dress. She was huddled up like a baby rabbit, and he was sure she was dead. He'd be suspected, of course. He'd have to ditch the case someplace, fast. He put his hand on her arm to squash her in again. The arm was warm. He jumped away. He closed the curtains and turned on the lights.

He couldn't put her back. She might be alive now, but soon she'd suffocate. It was a good thing he'd found her in time.

When he thought of that respectable type who'd shut her in the locker, he was amazed.

He got the plastic sheet he'd used to cover his Norton Atlas before one of his friends had borrowed the machine and smashed it to pieces. He spread the sheet over the bed and lifted the woman on top of it. He thought she looked fabulous, just like a dream. She seemed to be unharmed except for a mild discoloration on her left cheek, which might have been sustained in the packing. There was no blood that he could see. He thought he'd better do a complete check, to make sure she was all right. He took off her clothes. The dress was a bit weird, but she had some pretty classy underwear. Under the underwear was OK, too. He thought he might have some fun with her, while he was at it. He'd saved her life, after all: she owed him.

He was beginning to wonder what was going on—despite the warmth, she didn't actually seem to be breathing—when, accidentally, as he was running his hand through her hair, the side of his thumb hit two tiny, hard knobs of some kind and his problems were over.

The woman sighed and stretched out her arms. Her hands came softly around his back. Her eyes opened, her mouth smiled. She said, "Ooh, you're so nice."

Helen was curled up in her favorite living room chair when Edgar came in from work. She was reading the paperback she'd had to buy at the station; a nurse novel called *Summer of Passion*. She heard the car, the slam of the door, his feet crunching on the gravel of the driveway, the door being opened and shut. He called out, "Hi," going up the stairs. She answered, and read to the end of the paragraph: *at last Tracy knew that she had found the man of her desires and that this summer of passion would live in her heart forever.* Helen yawned. She put the phone bill between the pages of the book and stood up. Edgar was taking his time. Maybe he was running around the attic in circles, every time coming back to the empty sofa and not believing it. She didn't feel sorry. She felt mean-hearted, even cruel, and absolutely satisfied. Let him be on the receiving end of things for a while. It might do him some good.

The attic door slammed. He'd figured out she had to be the one to blame. He came thundering down the stairs and across the front hall. She put the book down on the coffee table. Edgar dashed into the room, breathing loudly. His hair was sticking up, as if he'd been running his hands through it. "Where is she?" he demanded.

"Who?"

"My experiment. You know what I'm talking about."

"Oh? It's a she, is it?"

"Where is she?" he shouted. "You get her back here, or you're going to wish you'd never been born." He took a step forward.

"Oh, no, you don't," she said. "You lay a finger on me, and you'll never see her again."

"What have you done with her?"

"That's my business. If you want her back, we're going to have to talk it over."

He looked defiant, but he gave in. She took up her stance by the red roses, he struck a pose in front of the Chinese lamp with the decorations that spelled out Good Fortune and Long Life. He said, "You don't know what you've done. It's a masterpiece. It's as if you'd stolen the Mona Lisa. The eyes—my God, how I worked to get the eyes right. It's a miracle."

A woman, she thought, *can get the eyes and everything else right without any trouble: her creative power is inherent. Men can never create; they only copy. That's why they're always so jealous.*

"What's her name, by the way?" she asked.

He looked embarrassed, finally. "Dolly," he said.

"Brilliant. I suppose you're going to tell me this is love."

"Helen, in case you still haven't grasped it after all these years—my main interest in life is science. Progress. Going forward into the future."

"OK. You must let me know how long it's going to take you to come up with the companion piece."

"What?"

This was her moment. She thought she might begin to rise

from the floor with the rush of excitement, the wonderful elation: dizzying, intoxicating, triumphant. This was power. There was even a phrase for it: drunk with power. No wonder people wouldn't give it up once they got hold of it. It was as if she'd been grabbed by something out of the sky, and pulled up; she was going higher and higher. Nothing could hurt her. She was invulnerable.

"I want," she said, "what you had—something nice on the side. A male escort: presentable, amusing, and a real stud."

"No way."

"Then I guess it's goodbye, Dolly."

"If you don't tell me—"

"Don't you dare touch me," she shrieked. "It's all right for you to play around in my own home, while I'm down here doing the housework, isn't it?"

"I don't think you understand."

"I don't?"

"It's just a doll."

"Pubic hair and nipples everywhere you look—that's some doll. And what about that twitch and switch business she does? That's a couple of giant steps ahead of the ones that just wet their pants and cry mama."

"It may turn out to have important medical uses. Ah . . . therapeutic."

"Good. That's just what I'm in need of."

"Helen," he said, "let's forget all about this."

"OK. It isn't that important to me. I can find a real man anywhere. But if you want your Dolly back, you can make me a perfect one. That's only fair. One for you and one for me."

"I don't know why you're so steamed up."

"I'm not that crazy about adultery, that's all. Especially if I'm the one who's being acted against."

"There's no question of adultery. In any case—well, in any case there's no moral lapse unless it's done with another person."

"No kidding? I thought the moral lapse was there even if you only did it in the mind."

"Let me explain it to you."

"Fine," she told him. "Just as long as you keep working at

my gigolo. And if there aren't any lapses, we're both in the clear, aren't we?"

The instant Dolly opened her eyes, Ron fell in love with her. Everything was different. Everything was solved. He'd never thought it would happen to him. He hadn't believed in it: Love. It was going to come as a big surprise to his friends down at the gym—they'd all agreed long ago that life was a lot better without women. They'd just have to get used to her. She was part of his life now. The fact that she was a doll he regarded as an advantage. You didn't need to feed her or buy her drinks or stop the car so she could keep looking for a rest room every five minutes. She was unchanging. The extraordinary skin she possessed cleaned and preserved itself without trouble; the mark on her cheek faded even before the smell of mothballs had worn off. A fresh, springlike fragrance seemed to breathe from her body. His friends would have to accept her as they'd have had to if he'd gotten married. That was what things were going to be like—like having a wife, except that not being human, of course, she was nicer.

That first day, he figured out how to use all the push buttons. He knew her name because she told him: she got right up close to his face, winked, gave a little giggle and whispered, "Dolly wants to play." She was so good at answering his questions that it took him some time to realize she was repeating, and that if he asked a particular question, she'd always give the same response, or one of several set replies. A similar repetitiveness characterized some of her physical reactions, but he didn't mind that. And when you thought about it, her conversation wasn't much more limited than most women's. She sometimes said something that didn't fit, that was all—never anything really stupid. And if she came up with the wrong wording, that wasn't her fault. It almost never happened. Her answers were so good and she was so understanding about everything, that he believed she knew what he was getting at; even if she was a doll, even if she wasn't real in any way. To him she was real. When he looked into her beautiful eyes, he was convinced that she loved him. He was happy. He was also sure that there were no others like her. There could be only one Dolly.

He told her everything. All about himself, what he wanted out of life, what his dreams of success used to be, how he'd grown up: all the things he used to think. He didn't know what he thought anymore and he didn't have any dreams left. He cried in her arms. She stroked his hair and called him darling. She said, "Hush, darling. It's all right." He believed her. He talked to her for hours. He knew that if she could, she'd speak as freely as he did.

Edgar applied for emergency leave from his job. It knocked out the holiday they'd been planning to take with the boys in the summer vacation, but he needed the time. He worked all day and most of the night. Helen brought up his meals on a tray. She tried to make comments once. He screamed at her. He shouted threats, oaths and accusations, ending up with a warning that if she didn't shut up about absolutely everything, he wouldn't be responsible. She smiled. She said in her gooey, peacemaker's voice, "What a pompous twerp you've turned into, Edgar." It was all out in the open now.

And he no longer felt guilty about his infidelities, mental or physical. It served her right. He wished that he'd been more adventurous, all the way back to the beginning, when they'd married: he wished he'd led a double life—a triple one. It was galling to be so hard at work, wasting the strength of his body and brain on the creation of a thing intended to give her pleasure. He could do it, of course; he had mastered the technique and the principles. But it was infuriating. It seemed to him now that there hadn't been a single moment when she'd been anything but a hindrance to him. She nagged, she had terrible moods, she wasn't such a wonderful cook, every once in a while she made a truly embarrassing scene—like the one at Christmas with his uncle—and she could wear really dumpy clothes that he didn't like. She'd keep wearing them after he'd expressly told her he didn't like them. And he didn't think she'd brought the boys up that well, either. They got away from her just in time.

He had needed Dolly in order to keep on living with his wife. If he couldn't have Dolly back, there was no point in going on. Now that there was no longer any secrecy, there was probably no more hope for his marriage. Still, as long as he could recover Dolly, there was hope for him.

When he thought about Dolly, he was ready to go through any trial, do any amount of work. He missed her. He missed the laugh in her voice and the look in her eyes when she said, "Let's have a good time. Let's have a ball."

He lost his concentration for a moment. The scalpel slipped. The voice box let out a horrible cry. He waited to see if Helen would come charging up the stairs to crouch by the banisters and listen. Nothing happened. Now that she knew, she wasn't worried. She'd wait and be silent.

At the beginning Ron was satisfied with keeping Dolly in his bedroom. But as he began to depend on her, he felt the desire to take her out. He'd found the buttons to make her walk and respond to his request for her to sit down or get up. A mild pressure on her arm would help her to change pace, turn a corner. Naturally the pink dress wasn't right for outdoor wear. He bought her a T-shirt and a skirt. She looked great in them. But the shoes were a problem: you had to try them on. He didn't want to spend money on the wrong size. He asked his friend Charlie, in a general way, what to do if you didn't know your size and couldn't put the shoes on to find out: if you were buying a present, say. Charlie told him to try L. L. Bean. "All you need to do," he told Ron, "is send them a tracing of your foot."

He had a lot of fun making the tracings with Dolly. He sent away for a pair of flat shoes. When they arrived, he walked her around the room in them for a long time, examining the skin on her feet at intervals. He didn't know what would happen if her skin got badly broken or damaged. He had no idea where he could take her to be fixed. He asked if the shoes felt OK; she said everything was just fine and she loved him—he was wonderful.

He sent away for a pair of high heels and some rubber

boots as well as socks, a parka, a shirt and a sweater, a pair
of corduroy trousers and a blue and white flannel nightgown
with ruffles around the neck. He also went out and bought
some fingernail polish. Her nails appeared to be indestructi-
ble, but the polish was chipping. The girl behind the counter
gave him a little lecture about the necessity of removing the
old polish before putting on a second coat. She sold him quite
a lot of cosmetic equipment. He thought, since he was there,
he might buy eye makeup and lipstick, too. "Does it come
with instructions?" he asked. The salesgirl sold him a book
with pictures and an expensive box full of tiny brushes.

He got hold of of an airport case that contained a roll of
traveler's checks and five silk suits. He won on the races and
after that, at the tables. Dolly was bringing him luck.

He took her out. People turned to look at her because
she was so beautiful, not because they thought something
was wrong. He felt like a million dollars walking down the
street with her. It was too bad that he couldn't get her to eat
or drink, because then he'd be able to take her into a
restaurant or a bar. But just walking along, arm in arm, was
nice. One afternoon he bumped into Charlie, who took a
look at Dolly and nearly fell over. "Jeez, Ron," he said,
"what a doll."

Dolly wrinkled up her nose and giggled. She squirmed a
little with excitement. Her eyes got bigger.

"Jeez," Charlie said again. "You going to introduce me?"

"Charlie, this is Dolly," Ron said. "Say hi, honey."

"Hi, honey," Dolly said. She put her hand in Charlie's.

Charlie said, "Oh boy. You been holding out on us, pal. Hi
there, Dolly. I don't know why my old buddy Ron here didn't
tell me about you before."

"We got to be going," Ron said.

"Oh, come on. You don't have to go, do you, Dolly?"

"Yes," Ron said. "Say goodbye, sugar pie."

Dolly twiddled her fingers at Charlie. She gave him a
breathy, hiccuping laugh and then whispered, "Goodbye,
sugar pie."

"Oh boy," Charlie said again.

Ron pulled her away fast. She clip-clopped beside him

quickly in her high heels, her hips swaying, her large eyes roving happily.

It hadn't gone too badly, but he didn't trust her for extended conversation. He figured they'd better put in some practice first.

He took on a job delivering goods for a friend. Everything was packed up in boxes. Maybe the boxes contained stuff he shouldn't know about. Normally he wouldn't care, but now he kept thinking about Dolly: what would happen to her if he got caught? She'd be found by somebody else, who'd take her away and keep her, just the way he had.

He stopped checking out the airport lockers. He began to look through the papers for legitimate work. Down at the gym they thought he was crazy—at least, they did at first. Word had gone around about Dolly; everybody asked about her. When was Ron going to bring her in to meet the gang?

He coached her for a while and then took her down to the gym. They all loved her. And they thought she was real. They said they could understand how Ron would want to settle down to something steady, if he had a girl like that. An older man named Bud actually clapped him on the shoulder and said something about wedding bells.

Ron wondered if maybe he could get away with introducing her to his sister and her family. He didn't see why not. He phoned Kathleen. She said sure.

"Only thing is," he explained, "she's on this very strict diet, so she won't eat anything. I thought I'd better tell you."

"Well, I can fix her a salad."

"No, it's sort of everything. She's allergic."

Kathleen told him not to worry. He put Dolly into the car, together with a change of clothes and her rubber boots. He drove carefully, thinking all the time that if they crashed, or if she were to cut herself in some other way, he wouldn't know what to do, where to take her. He didn't even know what was inside her; if she got hurt seriously, whatever was in there might all leak out.

Kathleen decided, as soon as she saw Dolly: she didn't like her. Her husband, Ben, thought Dolly was great. The children liked her too, but they didn't understand why she wouldn't

pat their dog, when it was evidently so interested in her and
kept sniffing around her. Ron grabbed the dog and kept it by
him. Later in the afternoon while they were walking along
the path by the creek, the dog ran ahead and almost made
Dolly trip over. At that moment Ron thought it couldn't
work: his friends at the gym were going to accept her, real or
not, but his family never would.

Before he drove off he sat Dolly in the car, walked back to
where Kathleen was standing, and asked, "Well? Do you like
her?"

"Sure. She's fine," Kathleen said. "A little dumb, maybe."

"But nice. She's got a heart of gold."

"I guess it's just—if people are really silly all the time, it's
too much like being with the kids. I start to get aggravated."

All the way back to town he felt angry. It wasn't right that
he should have to hide Dolly away like a secret vice. She
should be seen and admired.

The next day he took her on an expedition into town:
through the parks, into the big stores, around one of the
museums. The weather was good, which was lucky. He
didn't know how she'd react to rain or whether she'd be
steady on her feet over wet sidewalks. Of course, he didn't
know how a prolonged exposure to sunlight was going to
affect her, either, but she seemed all right. Her feet, too,
looked all right.

He took her by public transport, since that was part of the
idea. They rode on the subway, then they changed to a bus.
He had his arms around her as usual, when one of the other
passengers got up from the seat behind them, knocking Ron's
arm and the back of Dolly's head as he went by. Ron clutched
her more tightly; inadvertently he hit several of the control
buttons.

Dolly's arms raised themselves above her head, her eyelids
flickered, her legs shot apart, her hips began to swing
forward and back. "Ooh," she said, "you're so good."

He tried to find the switch. He panicked and turned it on
higher by mistake.

She went faster, gasping, "Oooh, you feel so nice, ooh do
it to me."

He fumbled at her hairline while people around them said, "Come on, mister, give us a break," and "That's some girlfriend you've got—can't you do it at home?"

He found the switch just as she was telling him—and the whole bus—the thing she loved best about him.

The driver put on the brakes and said, "OK, Mac, get that tramp out of my bus."

Ron refused. If he got out with Dolly before he'd planned to, he'd never be able to walk her to where they could get a cab or find another bus. "She can't help it," he said. "She's sick."

The driver came back to insist; he had a big beer belly. Ron got ready to punch him right in the middle of it and then drive the bus away himself. Dolly slumped against him, her face by his collarbone, her eyes closed. "It just comes over her sometimes," he said. That wasn't enough of an explanation, apparently. He added, "She had a real bad time when she was a kid."

The bus went quiet. Everyone thought over the implications of what Ron had said. The driver went back to the wheel. The bus started up again. Still no one spoke. The silence was beginning to be painful. Ron didn't know why he'd chosen that particular thing to say, even though it had worked—it had shut everybody up fine. But it left him feeling almost as strange as everyone else seemed to. By the end of the ride he'd begun to have a clear idea of the appalling childhood Dolly must have lived through. And he promised himself to take even better care of her than before, in order to make up for her sad life.

When his stop came, he carried her out in his arms. She appeared to be asleep. A few of the other passengers made hushed exclamations and murmurs of interest as he left.

He had to admit that there was always going to be a risk if he took her out in public. Driving alone with her in the car wouldn't be such a problem. He wanted to take her to the beach; to camp in the dunes and make love on the sands at night. He thought her skin would be proof against the abrasions of sand, the burning of the sun, the action of salt water. But he wasn't sure. The more he thought about her possible fragility, the more he worried. If he were hurt, even severely, he could be put together again: but could she?

Helen did the shopping, cooked the meals and began a thorough cleaning of everything in the house: the curtains, the chair covers, the rugs. She wouldn't have a spare moment to use for thought. She wanted to maintain her sense of outrage at a high level, where it could help to keep her active. She had no intention of breaking down into misery. She vacuumed and ironed and dusted. She washed and scrubbed. Once, just for a moment, her anger subsided and she felt wounded.

Edgar had done all that, she thought—he'd been driven to it—because she wasn't enough for him. She obviously hadn't been good enough in bed, either, otherwise he wouldn't have needed such a blatant type as compensation for her deficiencies. Her only success had been the children. She should really give up.

She caught herself just in time. She thought hard against despair, whipping her indignation up again. If things were bad, you should never crumple. Do something about it—no matter what. She stoked her fury until she thought she could do anything, even break up her marriage, if she had to. She was too mad to care whether she wrecked her home or not. *Let him suffer for a change*, she thought.

She could sue him: win a divorce case hands down. You could cite anybody nowadays. There had been a story in the papers recently about a man whose wife, without his knowledge, and—if he'd known—against his will, had had herself impregnated by a machine in a sperm-bank clinic. The husband had accused as corespondent, and therefore father of the child, the technician who'd switched on the apparatus. The fact that the operator of the machine was a woman had made no difference in law. And soon you'd be able to say it was the machine itself. Helen could name this Dolly as the other woman. Why not? When she produced the doll in court and switched on the buttons that sent her into her act, they'd hand the betrayed wife everything on a plate: house, children, her car, his car, the bank accounts—it would be a long list. If she thought about it, she might rather have just him. So, she wasn't going to think about it too hard. She kept on doing the housework.

Up in the attic Edgar worked quickly—frenetically, in fact—although to him it seemed slow. When the replica was ready, he brought it downstairs to the living room and sat it on a chair. He called out, "Helen," as she was coming around the corner from the hall. She'd heard him on the stairs.

"Well, it's ready," he told her.

She looked past him at the male doll sitting in the armchair. Edgar had dressed it in one of his suits.

"Oh, honestly, Edgar," she said.

"What?" He sounded close to collapse. He probably hadn't slept for days.

She said, "He looks like a floorwalker."

"There's nothing wrong with him. It's astounding, given the short time—"

"He looks so namby-pamby. I bet you didn't even put any hair on his chest."

"As a matter of fact—"

"You didn't?"

"The hair is extremely difficult to do, you know. I wasn't aware that all women found it such a necessary item. I understand a lot of them hold just the opposite view."

"And the skin. It's too smooth and soft-looking. It's like a woman's."

"Well, that's the kind I can make. Damn it, it's an exceptionally lifelike specimen. It ought to give complete satisfaction."

"It better," she said. She glared at the doll. She didn't like him at all. She moved forward to examine him more closely.

"And now," Edgar announced, "I want Dolly."

"Not till I've tried him out. What's this? The eyes, Edgar."

"They're perfect. What's wrong with them?"

"They're blue. I wanted them brown."

"Blue is the color I know how to do."

"And he's so pale. He almost looks unhealthy."

"I thought of building him so he'd strangle you in bed."
She smiled a long, slow smile she'd been practicing. It let
him know that she realized she was in control of the
situation. She asked him if he wanted to check into a hotel
somewhere, or maybe he'd stay up in the attic: because she
and her new friend planned to be busy in the bedroom for a
while.

"Don't overdo it," he told her. "It's possible to injure
yourself that way, you know."

"You let me worry about that." She asked for full instructions about the push-button system. She got the doll to rise
from the chair and walk up the stairs with her. Edgar went
out and got drunk for two days.

She tried out the doll at all the activities he was capable of.
She still didn't like him. He didn't look right, he could be
uncomfortable without constant monitoring, and his conversation was narrow in the extreme. His sexual prowess was
without subtlety, charm, surprise, or even much variety. She
didn't believe that her husband had tried to shortchange her;
he simply hadn't had the ingenuity to program a better
model.

As soon as Edgar sobered up, he knocked at the door. He
was full of demands. She didn't listen. She said, "Who was
the nerd you modeled this thing on?"

"I didn't. He's a kind of conglomerate."

"Conglomerate certainly isn't as good as whoever it was
you picked to make the girl from."

"I didn't pick anyone. Dolly isn't a copy. She's an ideal."

"Oh, my. Well, this one is definitely not my ideal."

"Tough. You made a bargain with me."

"And you gave me a dud."

"I don't believe it."

"He's so boring to talk to, you could go into rigor mortis
halfway through a sentence."

"I didn't think you wanted him to be able to discuss the
novels of Proust."

"But that could be arranged, couldn't it? You could feed
some books into him?"

"Sure."

"And he isn't such a high-stepper in the sack."

"Come on, Helen. Anything more and you'll rupture yourself."

"Reprogramming is what he needs. I can tell you exactly what I want added."

"You can go jump in the lake."

"And I want him to teach me Italian. And flower painting and intermediate *cordon bleu.*"

"No demonstration stuff. I can do a language if you get me the tapes, but they'll have to be changed when you graduate to the next stage. There isn't that much room inside for extra speech."

He was no longer angry or contemptuous. He looked exhausted. He made all the changes she'd asked for on the doll and added a tape of Italian lessons. She tried everything out. The renovated model was a great improvement. She felt worse than ever.

"Where is she?" Edgar pleaded, looking beaten, unhappy, hopeless.

Helen gave him the key to the locker.

Ron stopped taking Dolly to the gym when the boys began to pester him with too many questions. They pressed up around her in a circle, trying to find out what she thought of everything; that got him nervous and mixed her up. And then they started on him. What they most wanted to know was: where did she come from?

He had no answer to that, but no ideas about it, either. Lots of things—some of the most important things in life—remained completely mysterious. That didn't matter. It made more sense just to be happy you had them instead of asking questions about them all the time.

But one day while they were making love, instead of waiting for the end of the cycle she was on, Dolly went into a totally different one. Ron guessed that he must have given her some verbal instruction or physical signal. She started to do things he hadn't realized she knew about. He'd never done them himself, only heard about them. He did his best to keep up. She laughed with pleasure and said, "Does Edgar love his Dolly?"

"Who's Edgar?" he asked.

"Edgar's Dolly's honeybunch, isn't he? Dolly's so happy with her great big gorgeous Edgar, especially with his great big gorgeous—"

"I ain't Edgar," Ron yelled at her. He did something calculated to startle and possibly hurt her. She told him he was wonderful, the best she'd ever had: her very own Edgar.

It wasn't her fault. She didn't know any better. But it just about killed him.

He began to feel jealous. He hadn't wanted to think about how she was made—he'd assumed that she'd been made by machines. But now he had it figured out: she'd been custom-made for one person—a man named Edgar. It still didn't occur to him that this Edgar could have built her himself. He didn't think of things as being made by people. He thought of them as being bought in stores. She would have come from some very fancy place like the big stores where rich people bought diamond necklaces and matching sets of alligator-skin luggage, and so on. You could have all that stuff custom-made.

Someone else had thought her up. She'd been another man's invention. And Ron hadn't been the first to love her; he was sure about that. A sadness began to grow in him. The fact that she couldn't hold a real conversation still didn't bother him, nor that the things she said were always the same. What caused him pain was to hear her calling him by another man's name. He began to think he could live with that too if only in some other phrase she'd occasionally call him by his own name, too.

The sadness began to overshadow his love to such an extent that he thought he'd have to do something about it. He got the suitcase out from the back of the closet and went over the inside. There was a piece of white cardboard tucked into one of the shirt racks in the underside of the top lid. Someone had written a name and address on the card, together with a promise to reward the finder for the return of the case. The name matched the initials on the outside. The first letter of each was E; E for Edgar, maybe. People were so dumb, Ron thought. He'd never put a name or address on anything he was carrying around. Somebody could decide to come after you and clean up.

He put the card in his wallet but he still hadn't really made up his mind.

The next morning everything was decided for him while he was making breakfast in the kitchen. He'd cracked a couple of eggs into the frying pan and was walking over to the garbage pail with the shells. One of them jumped out of his hand. He scooped it up again and threw it out with the others. He meant to wipe a rag over the part of the floor where it had landed but the eggs started to sizzle in the pan. He stepped back to the stove. And at that moment, Dolly came into the room. Before he had a chance to warn her, she was all over the place—skidding and sliding, and landing with a thump.

He picked her up and sat her down on top of the folding stool. He asked, "Are you OK, honey?" She smiled and said she was fine. But he could see, in the middle of her right arm, a dent. He touched the center of the injured place lightly with the tips of his fingers, then he pushed the flat of his hand firmly over the higher edge of the indentation; he hoped that the pressure woud bring the hollow back up to its normal level. But nothing changed. The thing he was afraid of had happened.

"Dolly's hurt," she said. "Dolly needs a four-five-four repair."

"What's that?"

"Dolly needs a four-five-four repair on her arm."

"Uh-huh," he said. He didn't know what to do. All through the day he watched her, to see if the dent got bigger. It didn't; it stayed the same, but at regular intervals she reminded him that she needed to have the arm seen to.

He knew that it was dangerous to keep putting off the moment of action. He should find out what she'd need to have done if something worse went wrong. He could only do that by getting hold of whoever knew how to fix her; and then by trickery, threats, bribes, blackmail or violence, making sure he got the person to help him. If he could find somebody to teach him how to carry out all her repair work himself, that was what he'd like best.

When Edgar began his drive back to the house, Helen was sitting on the living room sofa at the opposite end from the male doll, who was teaching her how to conjugate the verb *to be* in Italian. While she was answering the questions put to her, she stared up at the wall, near the ceiling. She was already tired of him. The renovations had been minimal, she decided. Edgar wasn't able to program a better man, more intelligent, attractive. Perhaps no alterations would make any difference; maybe she just wanted him to be real, even if he was boring. Edgar evidently felt the other way: what he'd loved most about Dolly was that she was perfect, unreal, like a dream. The element of fantasy stimulated him.

For Helen, on the contrary, the excitement was over. Even the erotic thrill was gone. Owning the doll was probably going to be like driving a car—you'd begin by playing with it for fun and thinking it was a marvelous toy: but you'd end up putting it to practical use on chores like the shopping. From now on she'd be using the doll only as a routine measure for alleviating frustration. As soon as Edgar got Dolly back, there'd be plenty of opportunity for feeling frustrated and neglected.

She remembered what Edgar had said about the possible therapeutic value of such a doll. It could be true. There might be lots of people who'd favor the companionship of a nonhuman partner once a week. Or three times a day. No emotions, no strings attached. She thought about her sons: the schoolboy market. There were many categories that came to mind—the recently divorced, the husbands of women who were pregnant or new mothers, the wives of men who were ill, absent, unable, unfaithful, uninterested. And there would be no danger of venereal disease. There were great possibilities. If the idea could be turned into a commercial venture, it might make millions. They could advertise: *Ladies, are you lonely?* She might lend the doll to Gina and see what she thought.

"*Dov'è?*" the doll said.

"*Qui,*" she answered.

The front door opened and banged shut as Edgar's footsteps pounded through the hall. He was running. He burst into the living room and roared, "Where is she? I want the truth this time. And I mean it."

"The doll?" Helen said. "I gave you the key."

"Oh, yes. But when he got there, the cupboard was bare. There's nothing inside that locker. It's empty."

"It can't be. It's got two more days to go. Edgar, that was the right key and I put the suitcase in there myself. They aren't allowed to open those lockers before the money runs out. I put in so many—"

"But she isn't there."

"She's got to be. You must have tried the wrong locker. Or maybe the wrong part of the row. All those things look alike."

"I looked everywhere. I saw the right locker. It was the right one, but there wasn't any suitcase in it. If there was ever anything in it, it's gone now."

"Well, if it's gone," she said, "it's been stolen."

"It can't be stolen. No."

"That's the only explanation I can think of. That's where I put her, so she should still be there. I guess it happens sometimes that they get people forcing the locks, or whatever they do."

"How could you be so careless? To put her in a public place, where anybody could get at her."

"I didn't want to try to hide her in the house. I thought you'd find her."

"But how am I going to get her back?"

"I don't know."

"You'd better know. If I can't find her, Helen—it's the end."

"You could make another one, anytime."

"Impossible." He shook his head slowly and sat down in a chair. He still had his coat on.

Helen said, "I guess we could share Auto."

"Otto?"

"His name," she said, looking at the doll. "Automatico. Auto for short."

"Buon giorno," the doll murmured, making a slight bow from the waist.

Edgar said, "Hi," in a loud, unpleasant tone.

"Come sta?" the doll asked.

"That's all right, Auto," Helen said. "You can be quiet now. We've got some things to talk about."

"Bene, signora."

Edgar stared at the doll and snorted. "That's really what you wanted? The guy's a pain in the ass."

"He's getting to be very boring. He's about as interesting as a vibrator."

"I did just what you said."

"But I'm getting sort of sick of him. I always know what's coming next."

"I could program him for random selection—that's the best I can do."

"Maybe what I needed was you."

"It's a little late."

"It was a little late even before you started work on that thing. It began way back, with the computer—didn't it? Remember? When you stopped coming to the table. You'd make me bring in your meals and leave them. You can get a divorce for it nowadays: you cite the computer."

"I could cite Auto here."

"Not if you made him. I don't know what they'd call that—complicity or connivance, or something."

"I think I'll go out for a walk."

"What's your opinion of putting a doll like this on the market? It could become the new executive toy."

"Certainly not."

"Why not? We could make a fortune selling them. You think we should give them away?"

"Why stop with selling? You could run a rental service. Go into the call girl business: charge for every time."

"That's no good. If we didn't agree to sell them, they'd get stolen. People are going to want their own. Would it make a difference to let them out in the world—could somebody copy the way you do them?"

"Not yet. It's my invention. But if there's money in it, you can bet there'd be people after the process. Life wouldn't be worth living. We might not even be safe. That's one of the reasons I decided from the beginning, that if I had any success with the project, I'd keep it to myself."

"You said the dolls could have a therapeutic value."

"Yes, well . . . you had me cornered. The therapy was for me. Just as you suspected. I only wanted to make one."

"But all those techniques and materials—the skin, the vocal cords—everything: they could be used in hospitals, couldn't they?"

"No. It's all artificial."

"But it responds to touch and sound. If the dolls can do that, so could separate parts. You could fix almost any physical injury."

"Theoretically."

"It's possible?"

"In theory."

"Then you've got to. I didn't think that far, before. If it's really possible, it's our duty."

"Jesus God, Helen. You take the cake. You just do."

"Me? Who had the idea for this in the first place?"

"Not as a business."

"Oh, I see. That's what makes the difference, is it?"

Out in the hall the phone rang. Helen turned her head, but didn't move. Edgar said, "Aren't you going to get it?"

"I want to finish what we're talking about."

He stood up and went into the hall. She called after him, "Why don't you take your coat off?" He picked up the receiver and barked into it, "Hello?"

A muffled voice came over the wire, saying, "I got something belongs to you."

"Oh?"

"A suitcase."

"Yes," Edgar said quickly. "Where is it?"

"Something was inside it. Something kind of blond, with blue eyes."

"Where is she?"

"I'll do a deal," the voice said. "OK?"

"We can talk about that. Bring her here and we'll discuss it."

"Oh, no. I'm not bringing her anyplace."

"You don't understand. It's a very delicate mechanism. She shouldn't have been away so long. She could be damaged."

"She looks fine."

"She could be damaged and it wouldn't show. Internal injuries. I've got to have a look at her. She's supposed to have regular inspections."

There was silence at the other end. Edgar was covered in sweat. He couldn't think up any more reasons to tell the man why Dolly should come back. He said, "What's your name?"

"Ron," the voice told him.

"Well, Ron, you'd better believe me. If it goes beyond a certain stage, I can't fix anything. I've been worried out of my mind. She's got to come back to the lab."

"Are you the guy that, um . . ."

"I'm the designer."

"Uh-huh. OK."

"Now."

"Right. I'll be over." He hung up.

Edgar banged down the phone, threw off his coat and started up the stairs. Helen came out of the living room behind him. "Where are you going?" she said.

"He's got her."

"Who? What have you done with your coat?"

"A man that called up. Ron. He's bringing her over here now."

"Are you going out?"

"Of course not. Dolly's coming here."

"Well, come back and sit down," Helen said. She picked up his coat and hung it in the hall closet.

"I'm the one who knows about her," he muttered. "He can't do anything without me."

Helen pushed him into the living room and sat him down in a chair. She took Auto out, around the corner. She steered him to the downstairs guest room where Edgar's grandmother had once stayed after her leg operation. She stood him up in the closet and closed the door on him.

She waited with Edgar for ten minutes. As soon as they heard the car outside they both ran to the windows. They saw Ron get out of the car. He was wearing blue jeans and a red T-shirt. Helen said, "Well, he's a bit of a slob, but that's more the kind of thing I had in mind."

"What?"

"To wind up and go to bed with. That man there."

"Mm," Edgar said. He was wondering if he'd be strong enough to tackle a man like that, who looked as if he could knock people down. He began to think about what must have happened all the time Dolly was away. A man like that wouldn't have let her alone, once he'd seen her. Of course not. Edgar was ready to kill him, despite the difference in size.

Ron got Dolly out of the car. He handled her carefully. He walked her up the front steps. He rang the doorbell.

Edgar jerked the door open. The four of them stood looking at each other. Edgar said, "Hello, Dolly."

"Hello there, Edgar-poo," Dolly answered.

"How are you?"

"Dolly's just fine when Edgar's here."

Helen leaned close to Ron. She said, "I'm Helen."

"Ron," he said. "Hi."

"Why don't we all step into the house?" She led the way. She put the three others into the living room, brought in some coffee and sandwiches, and said she'd take Dolly into the next room.

"She stays here," Ron declared.

"She makes me nervous. I'm just going to put her in the guest room. You can come see."

Ron went with her. Helen opened the door to show him the empty room. She smiled at him. "See?" she told him. He laid Dolly down on top of the bed. He looked all around the room and stepped back. Helen closed the door.

Ron followed her back to the living room, where Edgar had changed from coffee to whiskey. Edgar said, "Want a drink?"

Ron nodded. He knew he had the upper hand, drunk or sober. Even over the phone Edgar had sounded like a drip.

Maybe he'd put Dolly together, but she was Ron's by right of conquest. Possession was nine-tenths of the law: that was what they said. Let Edgar what's-his-name try to take her back. Ron had a good left as well as a good right: he'd show this Edgar. And the woman was giving him the eye; he might be able to get her to back him up. Now that it occurred to him to notice, he knew who she was, too. She was the woman who'd put the suitcase into the locker.

Edgar began to talk, to plead, to describe the vague glimmerings of the dream he'd had: when Dolly had first come to him as a mere idea. He began to sound so desperate, he'd been so choked up at the sight of Dolly, that Ron pretended to soften. It didn't do any good to scare people too much while you were still trying to line them up; they could go and do something crazy. He said, "Look, Ed, I guess I can see how it is. You feel the same as me. But I can't let her go. You understand? I never thought I'd say it, but we're going to have to do some kind of a deal about sharing."

"Share Dolly? Not for anything."

"That's the way it's got to be. Or—you can make up your mind to go on without her. I'll just put her in the car and drive her out of your life again. It could be a long time till I needed to bring her back to you. You built her to last, didn't you?"

"I? Yes. I'm the important one. I'm the creator. You two—what are you? I created them."

"You create, maybe," Helen said, "but you don't appreciate."

"That's right," Ron told him. "You couldn't ever love Dolly like I do."

"I invented her, man. She's all mine—she's all me."

Helen said, "If you could hear what you sound like, Edgar."

"I sound like a man who's been treated badly. Helen, you used to understand me."

"Oh? That must have been nice for you. And did you understand me?" She stood up, went to the liquor cabinet and said, "You still haven't brought in the Cinzano. I'll get it." She marched from the room.

Edgar said to Ron, "It's true. You're the one who needs me."

"Right. That's why I'm willing to talk about it. You don't have to bother with this. You can make yourself another one. Can't you?"

"No."

"Sure. You make one, you can make two."

"I made a second one. It was no good."

"What was wrong with her?"

"It was a male replica. For my wife."

"Yeah?"

"It was her price for telling me where she put Dolly."

"No shit. And she didn't like it?'"

"It isn't real enough, apparently. She says she's bored with it."

"Maybe you're only good at them when it's a woman."

"No—I know what the trouble is. It's that I put all my best work, all my ideas and hopes, into that one effort. Dolly was the only time I could do it. I'm like a man who falls in love just once and can't feel the same about any other woman."

Ron didn't believe it. He thought Edgar wouldn't want to give anything to other people: that was the reason why he'd fail.

Edgar made himself a fresh drink. Helen, having found her bottle of vermouth, carried it to the guest room and parked it on the dresser while she took off Dolly's clothes, got Auto out of the closet and then stripped him too. She put him on top of Dolly, arranged both dolls in appropriate positions, and pushed the buttons behind their ears.

She took the bottle into the living room. She poured herself a drink.

Ron said, "OK. I get it. But you've got to see it my way, too. We do a deal, right?"

"I might go back on it," Edgar said.

"And then I'd come after you. And I've got a lot of friends, Ed. They don't all have real good manners, either. You think about that."

Helen drank three large gulps of her drink. She could hear the dolls. After a few seconds, the others heard too.

"What's that?" Edgar said.

"What's going on out there?" Ron asked. "Who else is in this house? You trying to pull something on me?"

"Let's go see," Helen suggested. She bounced toward the door and danced into the hallway. The raucous noise of the dolls drew the two men after her.

She smiled as she flung open the door to show Auto and Dolly engaged on what must have been round two of the full ten-patterned cycle: he whispering, "I could really go for you, you know," and she panting, "Oh, you gorgeous hunk of man," as he began to repeat, *"Bellissima,"* with increasingly frenzied enthusiasm.

Edgar and Ron called out curses. They rushed past Helen and grabbed Auto. They tore him away from his exertions. They got him down on the ground and began to kick him. They they hit out at each other. Helen took the opportunity to batter Dolly with the bottle she still held. Vermouth sloshed over the bed, onto the fighting men. Edgar slapped her across the face. The dolls, against all odds, continued to try to fornicate with anything and anyone they encountered, still mouthing expressions of rapturous delight, still whispering endearment and flattery; whereas Helen, Ron and Edgar roared out obscenities: they picked up any weapons they could find, laying about with pokers, shovels, baseball bats. Pieces of the dolls flew across the room. Springs twanged against the walls and ceiling. Reels of tape unwound themselves among the wreckage. And the battle went on; until at last—their faces contorted by hatred—husband, wife and stranger stood bruised, bloody, half-clothed and sweating among the rubble of what they had been fighting over: out of breath in the silent room, unable to speak. There was nothing to say. They stared as if they didn't recognize each other, or the room they were standing in, or any other part of the world which, until just a few moments before, had been theirs.

THE END OF TRAGEDY

Mamie joined Sal at Luigi's after the Friday evening performance. Sal was already sitting down, eating cherry cheesecake. Friday was the one day she went off her diet intentionally. Friday was also their payday.

Mamie didn't need to lose weight. She'd never liked sugary foods much, and though recently she'd started to drink at least one glass of something every night, she burned it off in the daytime. She was the pretty one: baby face and nice legs. Her only genuine acting talent was for screaming. It was a gift she hadn't known about until she'd gone to audition for a play based on a murder mystery.

"Can you scream?" the stage manager had asked her. He was leaning against a wall backstage, while he drank coffee out of a paper cup and watched the stagehands strike a set from the matinee.

"Sure, I guess so," she'd said.

"Let's hear it."

Mamie had looked around at the crowded stage, up at the lights and sandbags. She'd suddenly felt angry and desperate and as if she was never going to get anywhere in life or do anything. She screamed.

There was dead silence afterward. And a voice from somewhere said, "Mother of God, what was that?"

"You're hired," the stage manager told her. It was her first break. She played the maid who found the body at the end of Act I. She didn't have any words to say, only the scream. But she got so good at it that she made an impression on the management and they recommended her to the company where she met Sal. That was one of the few times she hadn't had to go to bed with someone in order to get a job.

Sal thought she was crazy. Sal had never slept with anybody for anything except fun. "It's because you're too

120

nice," she said, "and you don't think you can get what you want any other way."

"I'm not very good at anything else," Mamie told her. "I'm just beginning to realize: I'm probably never going to be very good as an actress."

"You certainly never will if you go around with that attitude. Think big, Mamie."

Sal was smart and a quick study. She could sing, she could dance; she had a strong vocal delivery. But she didn't have the looks. She'd grown up in Iowa, although you'd never have guessed she wasn't a girl from the city. With Mamie, you could still tell she was a country girl. If you listened hard to the accent, you could even place her: West Virginia. She hadn't had many friends growing up. At her school the girls had either felt sorry for her because of her family, or despised her; or, later, been jealous because of the boys. And she'd had only two other close friends in the theater besides Sal: one had married and the other had decided to stay with the telephone job she used to take between parts.

Mamie had been in hundreds of plays. She had even had lines in some of them. But neither she nor Sal had ever had the lead. They'd been in the company for five months while other girls had dropped out for various reasons: broken legs, proposals, suicide attempts, illnessses, parents who caught up with them, boyfriends who needed a girl who stayed put.

They'd studied cooking in Memphis, taken modern dance lessons in Peoria, attended a Japanese self-defense class in Kansas City. The Kansas City run had been the best. That was when Sal had asked Mamie to teach her the scream.

"We'd better go somewhere out in the open," Mamie had said.

They'd taken a picnic to one of the places they'd seen on the way to their classes. They had plenty of time on their hands, since Sal was trying to be faithful to a drummer whose band was playing in Chicago, and Mamie had just broken up with a tennis instructor and thought she was falling in love with their self-defense teacher, whom they called Mr. Moto because they kept disagreeing about his real name.

Before they ate anything, Sal wanted to hear the scream.

Mamie stood away from the tree under which they'd spread their tablecloth. She screamed three times.

"Now, you," she said.

But Sal's screams had nothing special about them. They were either completely ordinary, or sounded false. Mamie screamed with an immediate, thrilling release of mindless terror.

"How do you do it?" Sal asked. "Where do you start?"

"That's just it. You don't start. It comes all in one piece, from way down deep inside. It hurt my throat a lot in the beginning, but when I got used to it, I really started to enjoy it. Now it makes me feel good."

"It's horrible to hear. It's totally unnerving."

"If you practice, you'll pick it up. You've got to think it, sort of. And then you just let her rip."

"Let's eat first," Sal had said. And she'd never bothered with the scream after that. It remained the one thing Mamie could do better than other people.

Each of them had worked in companies where they'd been underpaid, not paid and run out on. The costumes had gone astray between one town and another, the props had broken, someone had sold the scenery and disappeared with the proceeds. The troupe they were with now was pretty well organized and it paid promptly. Friday was always a big occasion. They still couldn't forget the times when the funds had never come through. Mamie had even gone with men for money, although they hadn't put it that way and she didn't think of it like that. It had always been: "Can you lend me something till the end of the week?" The answer would be, "Sure, and how about coming out for a meal?" And afterward, going back to their place with them and somehow forgetting to pay them back, which she knew they didn't expect her to do anyway. She hadn't worried about it. There weren't many men she couldn't make herself feel fond of after a couple of drinks. Once in a while an evening would turn out to be a lot more unpleasant than she'd imagined, but that could also happen with the ones who seemed to be quiet and well behaved.

The main effect promiscuity had had on her was to make

her more susceptible to the idea of love. True love, she was certain, would wipe out other experiences. Love was like gambling in that respect—the big win canceled all your losses. And when true love came, she'd give up the stage. Love was the greatest role of all: everybody knew that.

Mamie came in late because she'd been trying to catch a last look at the man out front. She sat down opposite Sal and started to go over the menu, which she already knew by heart.

Luigi himself, whose real name was Harry, took their order. He winked at Sal. After he'd gone, Mamie whispered, "He's got a thing about you." Sal made her horror-movie face and let it freeze for a couple of seconds.

Their wine arrived, and the cannelloni. Sal said softly, "He was there again tonight. Same seat, same row. Talk about having a thing about somebody."

"Probably came in to get out of the rain."

"It isn't raining. You're the one he keeps staring at."

"How can you tell?"

"Well, can't you? Anybody like that looked at me, I'd be able to tell."

"I'm half-blinded by those lights," Mamie said.

She'd spotted him the first time he'd been to see the show. She noticed him because he looked just like the kind of man she'd always wanted to meet—the kind you saw in the movies and just as good-looking, except that he didn't look like an actor. He looked more real.

The second time he turned up, all the girls started to talk about him. It wasn't such a rotten show, but nobody could say it was *My Fair Lady*, either. The takings were low, the house was at least half-empty. It was strange to find someone coming back for more, especially a young man. This Friday night would be his fourth time in two weeks.

"I wish he'd make up his mind," Sal said. "If he's a talent scout, he should have known on the first night. And if it's anything else—well, I guess he ought to know that pretty quick, too."

"Do you get the feeling you're playing up to it?"

"Are you kidding? The whole back line of the chorus is knocking itself out. I'm exhausted. Aren't you?"

"I guess so."

"In fact, I'm so tired, I think I'm going to need some more of that cheesecake." She waited for Mamie to say something, but Mamie never made any comments about food on a Friday; that was their agreement.

Next day at the Saturday matinee he was sitting there again. And afterward, as Mamie came out of the stage door exit, he was waiting for her. She could see him clearly for the first time, standing close and directly in the light. He looked so wonderful she couldn't believe it: like an ad for something.

He said, "Miss Davenport? I hope you don't mind my coming backstage like this, but I really did enjoy your performance."

"Oh," she said. " 'Course I don't mind. It's nice when people come around to say they've liked the show. Makes us girls feel appreciated."

He smiled, showing beautiful teeth. "My names's Carter Mathews," he said. It sounded like a made-up name, but in her line of work she was used to that.

"And you know mine," she said. "Rhoda Davenport. Hi."

They shook hands. He asked her to come out for a cup of coffee, or a snack, a drink, or dinner, or anything at all. "Maybe supper after the evening performance?"

"That would be best," she said. "We're always kind of rushed on a Saturday."

"Fine. I'll meet you here after the show and take you out for a big meal somewhere, put you in a cab afterward. We can have a nice talk."

She spent the break between performances with Sal. They went to their Saturday cafeteria. Sal ordered a salad without dressing. She said, "Look, Mamie, I've been thinking. You don't want a salad?"

"Just the sandwich. I've got a date. I've got a date like you never saw in your life."

"What's his name?"

"Carter."

"His first name."

"That's his first name."

"Hotsy-totsy. You're in the big league now. I guess his last name's George or something? The nurse read the certificate backward?"

"You wait till you see him."

"What's he like?"

"Delightful, delovely, de works."

"Hair and eyes?"

"Uh-huh."

"Mamie, what does he look like?"

"Hollywood smile. Very kind of alert-looking. You know. Sort of light brown hair. Gray eyes. Real nice. I mean, honest." Just to tease, she kept back the information that he was the man from the audience.

They talked for an hour about Carter and whether he was going to be The One. Mamie tended to jump into affairs with both feet flying and then cry on Sal's shoulder for weeks about what a bum she'd picked, again.

Sal broke down and ordered the Roquefort dressing and a couple of doughnuts. She said, "I've been thinking: that girl we met last spring. Well—not girl. Suzanne."

"That's a cheerful subject."

"What I was thinking, was: I don't want to end up like that."

"No reason why you should. Just don't do it."

"I don't mean killing myself. I mean before—how discouraged she was; never getting any good parts, sleeping around with guys that said they'd help her and didn't. Hitting the bottle, taking sleeping pills, and a whole lot of other things too, I guess. Getting old, and nothing to show for it."

"It's a hazard of the profession, that's what they say. Never a dull moment, and no security. Isn't it better than being stuck behind a sink all day?"

"The older I get, the more I figure maybe the stove and the sink wouldn't be so bad. Especially when I wonder about

kids. I keep thinking, every once in a while, how nice it
would be."

"Well, find a man first. After that, it's up to you."

"Trouble is, I'm too used to thinking myself into a part."

"So, you might find out after about a year, you were sick of
that part and wanted to try another one. Where would you be
then?"

"Stuck,"Sal said.

He was there at the stage door, right on time, and took her
out to dinner. Everything seemed easy and relaxed. Then he
said, "I guess you know that what I was really interested in
was taking you out like this and having some fun. You don't
mind?"

She giggled, a bit drunk. She'd shot up to the ceiling on
half a bottle of white wine and felt great. She said, "Well, I
did sort of suspect something like that."

"But now that we're getting so friendly and I can tell what
a nice girl you are, I wonder if you could help me out. See,
that's why I was going around looking at shows in the first
place. I mean—not really, but I don't usually get the time to
enjoy myself like that, and I didn't know how to begin. I was
thinking of maybe going to a private detective."

"You've lost me," she said. "What are we talking about?"

"A job. But it isn't important. I'm just going to have to find
somebody at some point."

"What kind of job?"

"I guess you could call it impersonation, but there wouldn't
be anything shady about it. All completely straightforward."

"Guaranteed legit?"

"Oh, definitely. Like I said. Maybe it could be described as
entertainment; you know, sometimes a family gives big
weekend parties and they need a girl to make sure it runs
smoothly and looks good—sort of like being a receptionist."

Mamie put her glass to her mouth again. She'd met one
woman who had hired herself out as a go-go organizer for
parties back in the late sixties, and even back then it hadn't
been aboveboard.

"What I actually need," he said, "is just a girl who'll pose as my fiancée when I go to visit my cousins."

She could see from his face that he didn't mean anything weird, but she didn't know what to answer.

He said, "I guess it sounds silly."

"Why? Why do you need the fiancée?"

"It's to take the heat off of somebody else."

"What?"

"It's so dumb. There's this girl who was the girl next door when I was growing up. They kept trying to push us together all the time. And she's all right, just—we aren't interested in each other. Well, for a while I used to go out with her because it kept our parents happy and we could both go where we liked and do what we liked, and we'd just give each other alibis. Then she got mixed up with a married man, so she needed me as a cover. And I had my eye on somebody else too, so it was convenient for both of us. You see how the thing worked?"

"Sounds pretty good."

"Now she wants to get married to this guy, but her parents aren't going to accept it while I'm still on the loose. I know them."

"What about your parents?"

"They died three years ago."

"Both of them?"

He nodded. He looked so sad all of a sudden that she didn't want to ask him any more.

He took her back to her room and kissed her at the door. As he said goodnight he made her laugh, and, while she was still laughing, he walked over the threshold with her and kicked the door shut behind them.

"You've left the cab downstairs," she told him.

"Maybe you'd better come to my place," he suggested. "I could tell you all about how to be my fiancée. I'm too drunk to be dangerous. In fact, I'm kind of shy anyway. But I don't want to have to say goodnight yet."

She said OK. They got back into the taxi and went to his hotel. She marched straight to the side stairs and he met her on the landing after he'd picked up the key.

As soon as they got into his room it turned out that he wasn't drunk at all. Everything started to go a lot faster than she'd had any idea it would. They were in bed and she could see her clothes on the chair and on the floor. He wasn't a bit shy or even very nice. He was actually a little rough. She was still high enough not to be scared, but she bruised easily, and he was pinching and scratching and biting her.

"You're bruising me all over," she said.

He told her to shut up.

"You're hurting me."

"Shut up," he said, "or I'll hit you."

That shut her up. She turned her head to the side. She should have known better. It didn't happen often that she was completely wrong about a man, but every time it did, it seemed that it was the kind of stupid mistake she always made, and always her fault. The number of men, she thought, she'd said yes to just because she was lonely; and afterward you could tell they didn't even like you much. She was nearly ready to cry.

He lit a cigarette and put his left arm behind his head. He said, "You're very inhibited for an actress."

"What did you think I was—a professional?"

"I just thought, most of the actresses I know are into everything."

Including impersonation, she thought. Who knew what the story was there? He was obviously a good liar and better at acting than she was. His whole bedroom technique was worked out like a part: a solo part. A star part. He could screw for the Olympics.

She began to feel worse and worse. She reached down, found her slip, slung her legs over the side of the bed and put the slip on over her head.

"What are you doing?" he said.

"I think I'd better be going."

"What for?" He pulled her back and tried to turn her around. She didn't want to look at him.

"What's the matter? I thought you were having a pretty good time. Stick around. I'll introduce you to the whole of the repertoire."

She tried to stand up again, saying, "I think I might be too amateur."

"Come back here. I want to talk to you about being introduced as my fiancée."

"Oh? That's for real?"

"I told you."

"I thought maybe you'd just made it up."

"Why would I do that?"

"I don't know. People make things up sometimes." Sometimes they even said they loved you when you didn't need to hear it. That was a thing he hadn't done. Maybe he'd figured that with a girl like her, he wouldn't have to bother.

He said, "You've got the feeling you're being used, huh?"

"That doesn't worry me. That usually works both ways." What worried her was the lack of friendliness. It had reminded her of auditioning: when she'd be afraid that her performance was breaking up, and would become aware of the contempt aimed at her from out in the darkness where the judges were sitting, watching her go through her paces.

"Come back over here," he told her. "We'll get acquainted."

All of a sudden he was sweet and loving to her. He said he was sorry he'd upset her; he hadn't been with a woman for so long that he'd forgotten how to behave. She didn't believe that. And then she didn't care. She didn't even care that she was giving too much away. She knew all at once that he was The One, as she and Sal used to call it; so, everything was all right, even though she didn't know him very well yet.

They laughed about the job of posing as his fiancée. And he asked her about the other shows she'd been in. They laughed over them, too. He told her something about himself and his work; he was a lawyer. That impressed her. He'd come to town on business, to get someone to sign a paper for his firm; she kept forgetting the real name of the place because he liked to refer to the partnership as Eargerm and Stripling: the names had something to do with an office joke. They were the ones who had paid for the hotel the first time, when he'd been to see the show and decided that he wanted to have another look.

She told Sal everything, naturally. Sal said, "How you land yourself in these situations. He sounds like a real firecracker."

"He's great. He sort of took me by storm. I didn't think he was very nice at first. But he was just nervous. Can you imagine?"

"No," Sal said seriously. "He doesn't look in any way, even remotely, like the nervous type. Are you sure he's OK?"

Of course she was sure. She was sure for six weeks. And at the end of four, she was pretty sure she was pregnant. When he asked her to come back to his hometown to meet his relatives, she walked out on her job straightaway. "And afterward," she said, "I'll move, so you won't have to keep traveling back and forth. I could move in with you."

"Or we could find you another place of your own," he told her. "We'll see."

"All right," she said. By that time she'd know definitely about the pregnancy. By that time anything could have happened.

He did the driving. It was a new car and he owned it. His looks, his manner, his clothes: you could tell that everything about him was all right—respectable, coming from a good family that went back generations. He had his touchy side, but a lot of people had a funny temper.

It had been a long time since she'd been out of the city. She looked at the landscape moving past and felt happy. She loved him. She was convinced that this time she'd get married.

He didn't talk much except to tell her about the family she'd be meeting: Katherine and Waverley Chase, who had been his parents' best friends; and their three sons: Russell, Randall and Raymond. Russell had been married to Carter's cousin Julie. And for a few years when they were young, Carter and Julie and the Chase boys had all gone to the same school; until his parents had moved away.

"They're cousins by marriage?" she asked.

"They aren't anything. They were neighbors and my

cousin married into their family. But we'll be staying with them."

They checked in overnight at a motel that had an indoor skating rink as well as a large, heated pool and a room full of computer games. The restaurant wasn't bad, either; there was a help-yourself salad bar plus the usual waitress service. According to a cardboard notice on the table, private rooms were available for receptions; catering could be arranged. The building seemed to be the social center for several small towns in the neighborhood. Many of the diners were dressed up in Saturday night clothes: the women, in teetery heels, sported glitter and sleazy, backless dresses. One young couple, who were sitting in a booth near their table, had gone further than the rest and made themselves into living paintings: their hair had been striped with colors as bright as the feathers of a cockatoo, and made to stand out like sunbursts around their heads. The boy wore a great many earrings on each ear; the girl had a white, powdered face, red eye shadow, black lips and green fingernails. In every other way the two were rather conservative—dressed in black leather and not flaunting their unusual appearance but sitting quietly together, his arm over her shoulders. He was reading a copy of *Popular Mechanics*, she was doing a crossword puzzle in a book. They were relaxed and unself-conscious with each other, like an old married couple.

Mamie thought they were terrific. They looked like fun. But Carter said, "I'm surprised they let those two in. What a pair." And all at once she understood that the dividing line he had drawn between himself and a couple like that was final. He'd never associate with them. So now she too would have to keep at a distance from such odd-looking characters. He had already told her what subjects she should try never to to bring up when they arrived at the Chases'. "Don't do this," he said, and, "Don't do that."

They went back to their room. She put fifty cents in the bed massage and laughed hysterically as the mattress lumbered ponderously from side to side.

"What's it supposed to do?" she yelled. "That's the slowest bump-and-grind routine I've ever seen."

"Not so loud," he told her. "There are people next door."

"Come on over here. I've always wanted to try out one of these."

He went to brush his teeth. When he was finished, the bed had come to the end of its shimmy. He sat down on the edge.

He said, "I think we'd better get a few things straight. We'll be there tomorrow."

She looked up.

"Is your real name Rhoda?"

"My name's Mamie Hart."

"Mamie?"

"For May. The month I was born."

"Well, I guess it doesn't matter. I'll introduce you as Rhoda, if you like."

"Not enough class, huh? One of my aunts was called Maybelle—it's supposed to be French. We called her Mabel. And my grandparents were named Herz. They changed it to Hart."

"Is that a Jewish name?"

"Not that I know of. What is this? You want to see a racial purity badge or something? Sal used to say she got this kind of crap from people all the time. What would it matter, anyway, Jesus fucking Christ."

He slapped her hard on the right side of the head. "I told you not to use that word," he said. "If you want to trade obscenities in a barroom brawl somewhere, you go right ahead. That's the place for them. You're a little old for me to have to wash out your mouth with soap."

She burned all over. Tears had run from her eyes at the impact of the blow. She said, "You know what an obscenity is? An obscenity is what you just did."

"That's another thing. We've got to do something about your cheap dialogue. You've been in too many corny plays. You can't remember how real people talk."

"I've got a very good memory. I'll remember this." She pressed her hand against her face. Luckily he'd hit her fairly high up. She might have a black eye afterward, but the teeth were all right. The teeth were money.

"As far as I'm concerned," he said, "you can be anything,

and your name could be anything. It isn't me. It's some of the people you'll be meeting. I thought I'd better prepare you. Psychologically. You might find it hard to act your part."

"Oh? What part is that?"

"There's something I should have explained. I should have told you a lot of things, but it started to get harder and harder to begin. What I said about this other girl—well: it isn't exactly like that. It's a long story." He reached out to put his fingers against her cheek. She drew back a little. "That's all I need," he said, "you turning up there with a black eye."

"That's the only thing you're worried about, isn't it—that it's going to show? You don't care if you hurt me, only if it makes a mark."

"Sure, I care. I'm just getting kind of nerved up, now we're so near. I don't want to drag you into it. What I needed was a hired professional. I should have gone to a private detective and paid them to find somebody."

"What are you talking about?"

"My cousin Julie, who was married to this guy, Russell Chase; they call him Ross. We grew up together. She was my favorite cousin. Our families moved twice. When we were just kids, there wasn't anybody else around at all."

"You slept with her."

"You don't understand. She was my favorite cousin."

"And you slept with her."

"I guess so."

"You can't remember whether you did or didn't?"

"There wasn't any need for it. We were completely . . . but we did, yes. When we were in our early teens, really still children. She was actually only twelve. Then my parents moved. I didn't see her for years. We wrote to each other. I used to think . . . We didn't meet again till she was getting married. I was invited. And I knew then. I realized at the reception. I almost started to make a speech, try to take her away with me. When I kissed her, we knew that the wedding was a big mistake. I looked around and there were all our relatives and all of his, everybody dressed up, eating and drinking, the noise: I thought I was going crazy. I asked her to go with me right then, that minute. And she said, "I can't."

"So, you started sleeping with each other again," Mamie said. It was what she would have expected; she'd been in plays like that.

He sat up and lit a cigarette, took one long drag and then stubbed it out in the ashtray. He said, "We would have. I'd have made her get a divorce and it would have been all right. But we didn't get the time. They acted too fast. What they wanted was the money. It was divided in our family so there was part of it she got for her lifetime and then it reverted to me unless she had children. One of those complicated trust things. I don't know what old man Chase did with their own money and investments, but they needed somebody to bail them out and they had to get hold of it in a way that meant nothing could become mine before a certain time. Anyway, that's it."

"That's what?"

"That's why they killed her."

"They went to jail for murder and now they're—"

"They killed her and got away with it. Nobody else suspected."

"Carter, how can you know that?"

"I'm sure of it, positively. They were out mountain climbing. Said she got too near the edge. Well, I don't believe it. I got a so-called suicide note from her. Very good job of copying her handwriting, but it just isn't the way she said things. And she'd have used some of our special names, and so on. That was why I wanted somebody to try to get them to confess. I thought: if I got a girl to—"

"Me?"

"Maybe it was only Ross. Or maybe the whole family was in on it."

"Look," she said, "this is something crooked, isn't it? I've never been mixed up in anything crooked in my life."

"I told you, Rhoda, it's on the level. All I want is for you to get them feeling guilty and losing their nerve."

"But how could I do that?"

"Didn't I tell you? You look just like her. Like my cousin Julie."

"I feel sick," she said.

"You relax. They're the ones that are going to be feeling bad. You just enjoy yourself."

"Supposing these people did kill somebody—why wouldn't they kill me, too?"

"Because this time I'm here to protect you."

"Katherine," he said, "this is Rhoda Hart. Waverley, Randall, Ray, Ross; Rhoda."

Mamie shook hands with them all. She didn't understand why he'd used half of her real name and half of her stage name—especially why he hadn't done it the other way around, since Hart had seemed to be the one he'd had doubts about. ("I just forgot," he said later. "I was concentrating so hard on whether you'd be OK. And then it was too late.")

They sat down. She felt herself being sized up by the mother. One of the sons, the one named Randall, handed her a sherry. There was a log fire burning in the fireplace. Katherine Chase asked, "What part of the country do you come from, Miss Hart?"

"From the middle," she said. "Not really east or south. But not really anywhere else, either; in the mountains, from one of those small towns where everybody just wants to get out. It's funny how there's still any population in those areas. Nobody ever goes back."

" 'How you gonna keep 'em down on the farm,' " Waverley boomed. His wife swiveled her head around and glared at him.

"That's right," Mamie said. "Once you've had theaters and museums and nice restaurants and good clothes, going out and having fun—well, even if you want to settle down, it isn't going to be that kind of life again."

"You never go back?" Randall asked. He'd treated her to a long look and touched her hand as he'd passed the glass to her. The important one, Russell, had barely given her a glance.

"There are a couple of people I send Christmas cards to," she said. "But my family's all gone now." She stopped. There was a silence no one had foreseen. Suddenly it was absolute. She remembered her childhood. Her eyes filled with tears. She couldn't look at anyone.

"Yes, well," the third brother, Raymond, said. "Can I offer you a peanut? Or some of these things—what are they?"

"Cheese biscuits," Katherine said.

"They look like something that's been burned by mistake."

"No, thank you," Mamie said. She smiled at Raymond. And as she did, out of the corner of her eye she saw Russell look up and stare at her.

The lunch went well. Waverley and Randall both got moderately drunk. Everyone except Russell retired afterward for a nap. He stayed downstairs; "to do some work," he said.

The house was large enough so that she and Carter had been given separate rooms without having it look as though they were being kept apart for reasons of morality. Another one of his last-minute decisions had been to introduce her as a friend, not a fiancée. But their rooms were adjoining.

They went into her room and sat on the bed.

"If he's guilty about anything, he sure doesn't act it," she said.

"Why would he be guilty? He doesn't feel sorry and he isn't scared that anybody knows. I still can't make up my mind about the others."

"If guilt isn't going to worry him, there's no point in me being here. How's he going to go crazy if he doesn't care?"

"We've only been here a couple of hours. Give him a chance."

"I like the one that offered me the peanut."

"Raymond."

"But she hates me. And she's got me numbered, all right. The others don't mind. But men don't, usually."

"They do. They just show it differently." He lay back on the bed and closed his eyes. He said, "They're taking us out to the country club. Try to dance with all three of them."

"You sound like a real promoter. Like one of those greaseballs that come up and say: you want a girl, a nice girl, a schoolteacher, my sister?"

"I could hit you again, you know."

"And I could run downstairs and tell them all about your sneaky suspicions."

"I'd say you were just some girl I knew, who kept hallucinating. I can make things up pretty fast."

"But they've got to be thinking something. If I look just like her."

"Maybe they haven't seen the resemblance yet."

"Isn't it obvious?"

"Maybe not as obvious to them as it is to me."

"Do you have a picture of her?"

"No."

"Your favorite cousin? The girl you were in love with? You don't have a picture of her?"

"No."

"Why not?" He was trying to make her think he was falling asleep. "Why not?" she repeated.

"I tore them all up when she died," he said.

For a while she believed the torn-up picture story. He could make her believe in anything for a while. And then he'd come up with some other mystification and blame her for being slow to understand what he meant. He'd criticize or correct her about something: her speech, her lipstick, the fact that her skirt was wrinkled. He had chosen and paid for most of her clothes himself, but she sometimes wore the wrong shoes or tied an old kerchief around her neck. He noticed everything like that.

She followed his orders and reported back to him. There were periods when he'd grow sulky or quiet; he'd sit on the side of the bed in his room and fix his eyes on the wall. All she wanted now was to make love, but he'd move out of her embrace when she tried to hold on to him. He told her it was better not to, while they were still in the Chases' house.

"You could try rerouting it onto the boys," he said.

She didn't understand. One day he said, "You aren't doing very much to make them interested in you."

"What am I supposed to do? They think I'm your girlfriend, don't they? They aren't going to make a pass at somebody else's girl."

"Of course they are. That's half the fun, taking a girl away from somebody else. Tell them a hard-luck story. Tell them anything."

"I guess I should just lay it on the line and ask, 'How did you all kill Cousin Julie?' "

"For Christ's sake, no. Don't say anything about her."

"He doesn't like me, you know. Ross doesn't."

"First it was Katherine, now it's Russell. Everybody likes you fine."

"No. The others do, all right. But he hardly even looks at me."

"He's just a little under par with girls."

"He swept your favorite cousin off her feet, didn't he? He must have something."

"She was on the rebound. She was so hurt, she thought she needed a wet rag like that. She'd have turned down Randall and Ray."

"And you?"

"See if you can get him to confide in you. Be a good listener. You know—all those things your mother told you."

"My mother told me not to do it, but if I was going to do it, to make sure he had a bank balance first, and then get pregnant and go to his mother and cry."

"Was that what she did herself?"

"Of course not. She married for love and he didn't amount to anything. That's why she wanted me to have a better life."

She stood at the top landing and looked down. The carpeted and banistered stairways stretched away in three directions. Potted plants filled the landings with exuberant growth. They were placed in front of huge, ornate mirrors and thus appeared to spread their junglelike foliage twice as widely as they actually did. The stairs too ran up and down in the mirrors as you approached your reflection.

She'd always wanted to live in such a house. In the part of the country where she'd grown up there were a few houses like that, but she'd never been inside one. Once she got to the city, she saw a lot of beautiful places: never any back home. She hadn't been up on the knoll; her life had been down at the bottom of the hill in one of the little brick boxes near the railroad tracks. Her mother had been proud to think that one day the miserable thing would be theirs. That was what the family had hoped for.

It hadn't worked out that way. Her mother had died early. And Mamie had had no money behind her. She figured that if she had to drop down into real poverty, it would be better to do it in a big place, where nobody knew her. Possibly it would be more fun, too.

She'd been right. But it hadn't always been fun. And the shack near the railroad was Home Sweet Home compared with some of the places she'd been in: like that hotel where— if you got behind in the rent—the manager would come around and you could either pay up or go to the washrooms with him; and that didn't cancel the debt, either—he'd just defer it.

"Are you interested in fish, Rhoda?" a voice said below her.

She looked into the long mirror by her side and saw Russell's head reflected between the green leaves of rubber plants. She turned.

"To eat?"

"To look at while I feed them."

"Oh," she said. "Sure. What are they, in a tank?"

"In an aquarium. I'm taking care of it while the school's on vacation."

He drove her out to the deserted school. A light snow was falling. Indoors the radiators clanked. She hadn't been prepared for the different scale of the furniture, and was astonished at how small the desks and chairs were.

He walked her through into a hallway that smelled of sweeping compound. Paintings and crayon drawings, a thumbtack in each corner, covered the walls. Some of the pictures were hung fairly high up, but most had been set at the eye level of a small child.

They entered another, larger classroom where, at the far end, an immense aquarium stood in an alcove that had evidently been made for it. The water bubbled gently, the fish propelled themselves slowly around and around. It was the biggest fish tank she'd seen outside a bar.

"Some interesting specimens," he told her. She watched him shake the food into the water and check some gauges at the back. He wrote in a notebook, returned it to his pocket and moved his reading glasses up to the top of his head. Then he came and stood beside her, telling her the names of the various fish.

She put her fingers against the glass and pointed. "That one?" she asked. "And that one there?"

He put his arm around her. He kissed her neck. He slid his hand up under her sweater. She was about to push him away when she remembered Carter.

She let him keep going. He asked her in a whisper if it was all right. He didn't seem to her at all like someone who could ever have killed anybody. He seemed much more like a man who'd lost his wife and was dying of loneliness. She felt sorry for him. She said yes, it would be all right. He put their coats on the floor and flicked out the lights. She took off his glasses, which he'd forgotten he still had on.

On the drive back, he said something about not wanting to upset anything between her and Carter.

"Don't worry about that," she told him. "There hasn't been anything between us for a long time."

"I thought you and he were together."

"No. I think he was feeling kind of low after his girlfriend left him. He just invited me along for company."

She asked him to tell her about himself. He talked about marine biology and the study of ancient oceans from the fossil evidence.

He wanted to know about her, so she told him more or less the truth, leaving Carter out of it. Then she laughed. She said, "I can't get over those tiny little chairs and tables. It looked like pixieland in there. But it was nice." She hugged him. She felt that he was a friend now; there was no question that he liked her. He liked her a lot. It wasn't like the beginning with Carter, where she kept feeling afterward that in spite of everything, maybe she hadn't quite made the grade.

"Once," he told her, "when they were repainting in the town hall, everyone had to use the school for meetings. All the stuffed shirts and obstructionists had to sit at the kiddies' desks. They had their knees jammed inside and their thighs bulging over the seats, and there they were, muttering and scowling and trying to find someplace to rest their elbows. God, they looked silly. And still taking themselves so seriously, and the great importance of their jobs. That was wonderful. A friend of mine on the local paper even got some pictures, but they wouldn't let him print them."

Before he stopped the car, he asked her if she knew how to get to his room.

At the end of the week Carter took her back to town. It was supposed to be for a few days only; he'd return to his apartment in Chicago and let Ross make plans to start visiting her. Russell had said he wanted to see her before the geological conference he was to attend at the beginning of the month.

She still didn't understand what was going on. Sometimes Carter made her so confused that she stopped listening to what he was saying. She got ready to move out of town; that didn't take long. She had few possessions other than the clothes he'd bought for her. Now that she wasn't working and had the time, she couldn't fill up her days. She knew that she ought to think and plan ahead. But she just sat; or, sometimes, she went for walks.

She was out walking one day and started to feel so tired that she wanted to sit down. She was in the middle of town: not a bench anywhere in sight. Her head began to hurt. She saw a church in the distance and made for it.

She slumped into a pew at the back and kept her head

down. For a while she thought she was the only visitor to the building, but gradually she became aware that someone else had been up at the front when she'd entered. Sounds came to her of the person shuffling around, then footsteps went down the side aisle and stopped a few yards away from her. She moved her eyes slowly until she was able to see a long, black skirt and heavy shoes: some sort of man of God. She didn't raise her head because she knew that the headache would keep getting worse unless she stayed still. It hurt so much already that she didn't realize she might be sitting in an attitude of worship.

She thought of how, pretty soon, she was going to have to tell Carter about the baby. She had no idea how he was going to take the news. She herself was sometimes glad about it—since it was a hold over him; yet sometimes she thought no, he'd go to other women because of it. And when she considered that possibility, she didn't want to be pregnant.

The pain began to disperse, and at last went altogether. She got to her feet. On her way out she saw the man, a priest or preacher, standing near the entrance. He beamed at her. He'd probably thought she was praying, instead of just trying to get rid of a headache. She went back to her room and to the telephone.

Carter called her up. He told her to go out with Russell. He rented an apartment for her. She took the bus in to the theater to say goodbye to all the girls and moved, promising to send the address and phone number.

Carter paced up and down in the new place he'd found for her. He said he could no longer see how this scheme was going to work out. He didn't know what to do. He'd had a dream about Julie in which she'd stood at the edge of a mountain view and pointed at him and said he wasn't fulfilling his promise.

He kept her up late talking when she was falling asleep with weariness. He was impatient and abrupt and made her cry. One evening she said she couldn't stand any more. "I keep doing just whatever you say," she told him. "I'm beginning to think this whole thing is nothing but lies. And you aren't nice to me."

"I want you to ask him over for the weekend or something. His hours are pretty free outside of those meetings and research trips."

"I think I'm pregnant," she said.

He was delighted. He said, "Ask him over and tell him."

"It's yours. You know that already."

"But he won't know."

"Carter, why do you want all this?"

"They killed her. I keep telling you. Don't you believe me?"

"I believed you when you said you liked me, and when you told me the story about the girl next door, and I believed you about your cousin. Now what else do I have to believe?"

"And that they murdered her."

"And how they pushed her off the mountainside, sure. But most of all, I believe it that you hit me in the face that time. And I think you're planning something bad for me."

"Not for you," he said. "Nothing bad for you. For them."

"But everything's changed now."

"It's perfect. You get married to him, and then we've got him."

"How?"

"He'll trust you then."

"Carter, if he really did kill anyone, maybe I'll be in danger."

"They killed her for the money. You'll be fine."

"Listen: you're a lawyer. If I get married to him, the baby's going to be his—isn't that right?"

"What did you want to go and get pregnant for in the first place? You aren't usually so careless, are you?"

"I guess I forgot."

"Or maybe you were following your mother's advice and thought I'd marry you myself."

"I should never have told you that. It isn't nice of you to use things against me. You shouldn't do that to people you love."

"Who's talking about love?" he said. "Pick up the phone, Rhoda. I think you should give Ross a call."

"Maybe I should tell him everything."

"Don't try it. I told you: I'm a lot better at this kind of thing than you'll ever be. You just do what I say, and we'll come out of it OK in the end."

"You mean, we'll get married?"

"Eventually, yes. Of course. Didn't you know that?"

"But if I'm already married to him? A divorce takes a long time."

"I'm the lawyer, remember. I can take care of that side of things." He dialed the number for her and pulled her to his side. As he gave her the receiver, he put his hand over her left breast and kept it there. Her heart thumped so hard that she couldn't think straight. She laid her hand over his and turned to look at his face. He mouthed words to her. She said, "Hello? Could I speak to Russell Chase, please?"

When she told Russell he smiled a little, grinned, and then threw his arms around her. She burst into tears of remorse.

He took charge. He talked and talked: about how this was the best way, in some countries it was still considered the only way to get married, and he was sure he'd be good with children; he'd always thought babies were very interesting—he'd always wished that he hadn't been the youngest in his family.

He made her blow her nose and told her that they'd go down to the town hall in the morning.

"Did you want a church wedding?"

"No," she gasped, "definitely not a church wedding. It wouldn't feel right. Tell you the truth, I've never felt easy about church. Where I come from, it's all Holy Rollers and pointing the finger of sin, and the whole thing makes you feel kind of horrible even before you've thought of doing anything wrong."

"That's just as well. I wouldn't want to go through it a second time, either. I don't know if you know: I was married before. There's so much we've got to catch up on, find out about each other."

"Carter told me," she said. "And she died in some kind of accident?"

"Yes."

"I'm sorry."

"Yes. I'll tell you someday. I guess everyone takes it for granted in peacetime that only old people die; but it isn't true. Anybody can die, from any cause. It's a shock when it happens to someone your own age, or younger."

He asked if there was anyone from her family she'd want to invite to the ceremony. She shook her head. She said, "My family isn't—wasn't—anything like yours. I mean, you can tell I'm not a college girl. But my father was an honest working man. He had a job with the railroad. It's just that after my mother died, he started to drink a lot. So, finally one night he drank too much and slipped and hit his head. I don't think they were the kind of people your mother would approve of much."

"Mother is marvelous, but she's a terrible snob. You must have noticed. She's a snob about everybody and everything. Just ignore it."

She agreed to all the wedding plans. A few hours later, however, she thought again. She phoned Carter.

"Stop crying," he snapped at her. "I can't hear half of what you're saying. And anyway, I told you already: not on the phone. I'd better come over." He hung up immediately, without saying goodbye.

She felt tired and seasick and as if she'd never be able to stop wanting to cry. When she opened the door to him, he blew smoke into her face from his cigarette and didn't kiss her or touch her. "Sit down," he ordered. "What is it, Rhoda?"

"I can't go through with it."

"Doesn't he like the idea of being a father?"

"He loves it. He's so nice. I can't do it."

"He's so nice, he pushed Julie out into empty space and watched her fall a hundred miles down, without batting an eyelid."

"It's your baby. Don't you have any feelings about it?"

He crossed to the sofa, tossed his coat over the arm and sat

down next to her. He put out what was left of his cigarette.
"You know why I chose you," he said.

"Sure. You knew I needed the money."

"I knew you needed the money, and you'd need me, and you'd get used to nice things fast. And you look right."

"Like her," she said.

"Only a little. Only the same general type, and that's how people spot resemblances: by the type. If anyone wanted to compare you both detail by detail, you actually look completely different. And you're a lot prettier, of course."

"But you loved her."

"Not really. A little. It's nice to have cousins—somebody who's midway between friends and brothers or sisters. She didn't deserve that. They did it because of the money. We were supposed to inherit it fifty-fifty, but then my grandfather . . . You know, sometimes people try to be so helpful when they should just keep their big mouths shut and not go telling about some escapade you thought was amusing. Old people don't always have the same kind of humor. But she was fine; she turned up trumps—said we'd split it just the way he intended in the first will. And she was all ready to hand it over when the Chase family decided to take a skiing holiday way up in the mountains. That's another thing: she was really good at all those winter sports. She'd never have lost her footing. They thought it was such a good choice because it would look natural: but not to me." He put his elbows on his knees, his head in his hands, and sighed. "That's the way it was. They cleaned up. Pulled their lousy bank out of the red, and everything. But I swore to get it back. I didn't know exactly how. What I had in mind was getting some kind of evidence to threaten them with."

"Like what?"

"I don't know anymore. I was going to play it by ear. Then I fell in love with you. I didn't mean to. I never fall in love with anybody. It's ruined everything." He leaned over and laid his head in her lap. He sighed again, loudly, several times. It sounded like sobbing. She smoothed her hand over his hair.

"Are we going to get married?" she asked.

"Afterward."

"After what, Carter?"

"After we get the money." He sat up and reached for another cigarette.

She got to her feet. She said, "You couldn't love me and let me sleep with another man. You couldn't want me to get married to another man. Not if you loved me."

"It's only for a little while. And you'll still be mine. Tell him you can't, because of the baby. Maybe you shouldn't, anyway. It might be bad for you."

She started to answer and began to stammer. She couldn't go on. He took her arm and pulled her down beside him. "Think of the life we'll have afterward," he said. "And our kids, too. All the things we can do."

"But we could be happy now. We could have a good life. Why can't you forget about it?"

"Why should I?" he shouted. "Why shouldn't I have all the good things I was meant to have?"

"You can work for them. We both can."

"Not that kind of money. That kind you've got to inherit."

"It's too bad you're a man. Otherwise, you could marry for it."

"Oh, I could still do that. Couldn't I? Everything in perfect working order."

"You wouldn't."

"Too much time and effort. This way's better."

"Not for me. If we love each other, we should do it the right way."

"Get married, be poor, and get to be as unhappy as everybody else?"

"Lots of people are poor. I grew up that way. It wasn't so bad."

"Wasn't it?"

"It was better than what you've got in mind. Anyway, you talk about being poor, but you've got a good job."

"It takes me everything I earn just to keep up the payments on my apartment. Christ, I don't even like the place. When would we ever take a vacation, or get a house? And with a baby, too?"

"But I'll be his wife. Every night—"

"Well, you did it once. More than once."

She'd forgotten what she had or hadn't done, or how often. She remembered that he'd made her so miserable and angry that she'd have done anything.

"That isn't important," he added.

"Marriage is even more. It's more than you think. I've seen it happen with a lot of girls. You think it's just like an official version of the usual thing, but it isn't."

"It's only the piece of paper and how people think about it. Society's approval."

"It's everything," she said. "It's the whole family. It's stronger than you've got any idea. And no amount of money is worth giving up happiness for."

"It's mine," he insisted. "And I can't take that job much longer. I've worked my ass off in that place. When you start out, they work you right around the clock. They work you into the ground."

"But that's over. You told me, you're going to be a junior partner."

"Big deal. So I can have thirty more years of working myself into the grave for them. I want to get out. All the way out, and be free."

"Being a lawyer," she said, "is a nice job, well paid, steady."

"Nine to five every day, to the end of my days?"

"I don't understand what you think is so bad about it."

"You saw their house—that's only part of it. And the bastards have thrown more than half of it away. Russell gets through money like a drunken sailor. Every minute we waste, there's less of it left. Do this for me, Rhoda. Please. I promise it'll be OK in the end."

"How can it be? How are we even going to see each other if I'm married to somebody else?"

"I'll work something out," he said. "And don't look so sad. Think of it like going into enemy country as a spy during wartime. You've got to be brave."

"And be a good actress," she said. She gave up. She gave in. She married Russell.

*   *   *

When she was seven months pregnant, Mamie thought she couldn't take anything any longer. She missed Carter all the time. She had no friends except Russell, and he—she was now sure—didn't intend, as he had first promised, to move out of his parents' house. "It's so comfortable," he said. "Plenty of room for all my specimens and for the periodicals, too. We'd need a huge place if we moved. Don't you like it here?"

"I'm like a guest. I never even wash a dish."

"You're the first girl I ever heard of who liked washing dishes."

"You know what I mean."

She asked if she could go back to town just for the weekend to see a friend. He agreed straightaway. He trusted her completely. When they had signed the joint insurance papers, he'd had himself insured for so much that if he died, she'd never have to take a job again. She'd be a rich woman. It worked the other way around too, of course, but that was only sensible if he was ever going to find himself in the position of having to bring up a child on his own.

She made a reservation at the kind of hotel she'd never stayed in before. And she started to telephone Carter before she'd even unpacked. She couldn't get through to him either at his apartment or at the office. She tried for hours, then she went out for a walk.

It was a cool day. In the park the flowers looked wrong for the time of year. Mothers and baby-sitters, dressed in coats and sweaters, sat on the benches while the children they were looking after played nearby. She should have been feeling good.

She thought of sitting down on a bench, but kept walking. Her fur coat was unbuttoned, the large swell of her body bulging through the opening, but she didn't feel cold; the heat generated by the fetus added to her own warmth. If she sat down anywhere, she knew someone would come up to her and ask about the baby. Now that it was so prominent, everyone did. They were just being friendly, but she sometimes wanted to say, "Go take an interest in somebody's else's stomach."

She walked down into a section of town she knew from touring days. She thought about Sal, who was in another company now. She remembered the name of the company. It would be nice to see Sal, she thought. She bought a newspaper; there, among the ads on the theater page, she found the address: the place where Sal's show was playing. She waved down a taxi, went to the theater and bought a ticket for the orchestra. Now that she had money, she didn't think twice about buying an expensive seat.

The place was nearly deserted. A few old ladies, sitting two-by-two and wearing their hats, were bunched together in the front rows. She remembered those matinee audiences: how there were always two old ladies, usually in the front row, who would talk to each other all through the show in voices just as loud as your own.

The play was terrible. It was about an American sculptor living in Italy with his wife. Once he'd been good, but now he was reaching middle age and losing his talent, and he'd fallen in love with the Italian girl who was acting as his model. In the second act he had a long soliloquy about art and Michelangelo and the reasons why he'd wanted to go to Italy and why he felt such disdain for himself in the face of all the great works around him. Several times Mamie was afraid she was going to fall asleep, but she was kept awake by the thought that she'd see Sal come onstage again. Sal was playing the maid; she didn't have anything to say other than "Sì, signore" until the last act, where she made the most of a speech in broken English, telling the sculptor that the signora had left and there was a letter she'd wanted him to have.

Mamie went backstage afterward. Sal came bounding out the door with her arms open.

"I saw you," she yelled. "My God, I couldn't believe it. I nearly dropped the coffeepot again. Jesus, Mamie, you're pregnant."

"I couldn't get out on the mat with Mr. Moto anymore, that's for sure."

"Mr. Moto, oh, my God: that was such a long time ago. Where was it?"

"Kansas City. It was the only sport I was ever really good at. Except dancing, of course—but that's an art. That's what Mrs. Beebie kept saying."

"Hell, yes. I remember. I was always a total bust at that karate, but I had a big crush on him."

"Me, too. I just wish I could remember his real name. Are you doing anything before the next show?"

"You're kidding. I've got enough spare time to learn Outer Mongolian."

"Let's go eat," Mamie said. "My treat."

"You bet it is, in that coat. What is it? That's the minkiest mink I've ever seen."

"It's a sable," Mamie said. She could feel herself smirking a little. *And why not*, she thought.

They went to a restaurant Sal picked out. "The sky's the limit," Mamie said. "Anything you like, and have it twice. If you're on a diet, this is the day to forget it."

They went through the menu and ordered. Sal started on a bottle of wine, which Mamie refused, saying that it made her feel sick. "And being in very smoky places," she added.

"And the ring!" Sal exclaimed. "Oh, wow. Eat your heart out, Elizabeth Taylor."

Mamie stretched her hand across the table so Sal could get a better look. "I thought you were great in the play," she said. "You were the only good thing. That big speech in the second act—"

"When he gets the throb in his voice, uh-huh. He's such a jerk. But this time it isn't his fault. I couldn't say those lines any better. And the empty house isn't much help. I'm afraid this one's just your archetypal turkey."

Sal began to talk about herself. Mamie pumped her with questions until they'd eaten their way to the dessert. Sal said, "What have you got in there—triplets? And I was the one that wanted kids. So how's old Carter?"

"It isn't Carter. It's his cousin's ex-husband. That's how these things happen: shazam."

"How about that. I could use some shazam myself for a change."

"Things bad?"

"I'm sort of down around low tide."

"If it's money, ask."

"No, the money's only the way it always is. I guess it's just this time of year. Thinking about love. You know. Even now it's gotten so cold out. You can't help thinking."

Yes, Mamie said, she knew.

Later in the evening, when Sal was making up to go onstage, she tried to get hold of Carter again. But he must have been out of town for the weekend. She had to go back without seeing him.

She thought about him all the way to the house. She wondered if he was alone, or with somebody else. There was no shortage of women in town. When she remembered how the girls used to talk backstage, how they were all dying for it, she was sure he'd be with someone, another girl: somebody better. And maybe he'd be saying he loved her, bringing her flowers, buying her presents.

He'd only ever given her one thing, at the beginning: a key chain with an enameled butterfly at the end of it. He said he didn't believe in presents. All the clothes he'd bought her for the visit to the Chases had been in the nature of a theatrical wardrobe; they were for business and professional purposes.

She loved the key chain, but he'd never bought her anything else. She hadn't expected him to, yet most men would have. She didn't think about it until one day when they were passing by a jeweler's shop and she lingered to look in.

"This is cheap stuff," he said.

"That's the kind I can afford." Her eye ran over the watches, clocks, plated cups, flashy earrings and chunky fake bracelets. Then, in one of the front corners she saw a collection of silver charms. She leaned closer.

"Come on," he told her. She switched her attention away from a silver heart and was suddenly looking at a charm made of the two masks of drama, comedy and tragedy.

"Look. Look at that," she said. He admitted that they weren't bad, but he wanted to move on.

She said, "Let's go in. Just to see how much."

She walked in without him and he followed. When the man behind the counter brought out the charm, she still thought it was perfect, and it wasn't expensive. That was the point where Carter should have offered to buy it for her. He shook his head. She bought it herself.

After they were out on the street again and had walked halfway to the restaurant they were going to, she took the charm out of its box and examined it.

He snatched it from her hand, stared at it, and began to tug at the two halves.

"What are you doing?" she asked. "You'll break it."

He wrenched the two masks apart and threw one into the street.

"What are you doing?" she said again.

"I don't like the idea of you wearing that unlucky thing." He handed her the piece that was left: the comedy mask.

"But it looks silly now. They're meant to go together. It's one of the things you've got to have in pairs. Like men and women."

"Sometimes I think we'd be better off with only one of those, too."

"What am I going to do with just one?"

"I don't know. Wear it as an earring. You could start a fashion. One earring."

"That's already a fashion."

"OK, start another one. The hell with it."

She stepped off the curb and searched up and down, trying to find the other mask again, but he took her by the hand and yanked her along with him, away from the place where she'd heard it land.

"You don't buy me anything," she said, "and when I get something for myself, you tear it to pieces."

"I'll buy you something else."

"But why did you do it?"

"What do you want a bad-luck thing like that for?" He dragged her into a large, expensive store, looked around aggressively and grabbed a silk scarf that was draped over the handle of a crocodile bag. It was part of the display.

"You like that?" he asked.

"Well, of course," she said. It was one of the biggest silk scarves she'd ever seen and covered with prints of flowers in all different colors. "But it's too expensive."

A salesgirl was at his elbow straightaway. She'd left her counter as soon as she'd seen them touching the scarf. He asked the price and Mamie was right—it cost more than a good dress would be. He bought it for her.

It became her favorite piece of clothing. She wore it around her neck or shoulders, or tied around her head, or at her waist. Russell liked it, too; it always paid, he said, to buy the best. And Mamie thought: *Everything always pays, if you've got the money for it.*

She still hadn't seen him by the summer. And then the baby was born.

She was entirely absorbed in her child, as if hypnotized. At times she was also unhappier than she had been since she'd left West Virginia. It was like the year when her mother and father had died. She would cry for long periods. She didn't want to go out of the house. It wasn't that she was afraid, just that she didn't want to leave the baby. Russell was understanding, and Katherine suddenly seemed sympathetic—still cold and reserved, but she didn't lecture about her own experience as a mother or attempt to criticize: she tried to be encouraging and to talk about practical, ordinary things.

At night Mamie had anxious dreams. She kept remembering her mother, who had never talked about anything that had to do with the process of reproduction, and hadn't even told her daughter the facts of life; Mamie had had to get the information from school and gossiping with friends. But now she wondered about her mother: *Did she feel like this? Did she walk up and down with me to stop me crying; did she sing me to sleep?*

Russell spoke to her about taking a winter vacation in the sun somewhere. The grandparents started a savings account for baby Waverley, whom they called Bobby. And, for the baby's sake, the grown Waverley, her father-in-law, gave Mamie some stocks and shares, including shares in the bank. She had a private income now, as well as her bank account.

Sometimes Russell would ask her to lend him money until a check came through. She had plenty; she didn't mind. But one day Randall told her that somebody ought to have a word with Ross about his gambling.

"It's just a little roulette, isn't it?" she said.

"It's always a lot, and he keeps thinking he's got this system. He's been like that ever since school. I think he should see a doctor about it. It's like throwing it away. Julie—"

"Yes?"

"Julie tried to stop him, but she couldn't, either. Maybe you can. Now that he's a father—well, he should show some responsibility."

She asked Russell later, "Do you gamble a lot?"

"Just for fun."

"Randall told me I was supposed to get you to stop."

"He's probably right. But it's the excitement. You can get hooked on it."

"It doesn't matter, as long as you break even. You wouldn't keep playing if you lost all the time, would you?"

He said, "One loss never counts when you know you can win it back a hundred times over on the next round."

"You lose a lot?"

"Don't worry about it. I've got plenty to pay with."

"Some of those casinos are run by pretty tough people, you know. I've heard they can actually hire men to take out a contract on customers that don't pay up."

"But I always pay up," he told her. He sounded completely relaxed about the subject. She shrugged and said that everything was all right, then.

As soon as she was through with her special exercises and the checkups, and felt that she was back to normal again, she asked to go into town to show the baby to Sal. She did mean to see Sal at some point, but the real reason for the trip would be to meet Carter.

*   *   *

She didn't take the fur coat or the diamond. This time she wore corduroy pants and a parka. She carried a duffel bag for her clothes and a neck sling for Bobby.

She took him to the theater first, to show Sal. Sal was speechless for a moment. And then she changed expression in a way Mamie had never seen outside the movies: she looked transfigured. She wanted to hold the baby. She called the other girls over. Three of them, including Sal, cried when Mamie got ready to go. They didn't want him to leave.

She went to a big department store she knew, had a snack in the restaurant and then moved to the ladies' room, and on to the large entrance hall next to it, where there were chairs and couches. She sat down and changed Bobby and breast-fed him. She kept looking at her watch, but it didn't matter. Carter would wait.

She walked. And she didn't begin to hurry when she saw that she was getting near the park.

Carter was sitting on one of the benches. He was smoking a cigarette. He looked as if he'd been waiting a long while. He was thinner than the last time she'd seen him. He stood up as she approached. "Did you have to bring the kid?" he said.

"I wanted to show him off to my friends. They loved him. And besides, I still need to feed him." She sat down on the bench. "You don't have to look if you don't want to. You might turn to stone or something."

He sat down again and took a quick look at the baby, asleep after its meal. He grunted. He said, "You didn't find out about the money."

"How can I ask? I don't want to get him mad at me. You don't know what he's like. He's got this way of . . . He doesn't like to be criticized and if you say anything, you can feel his trust in you sort of seeping away. And then you're the one that feels bad."

"I can picture it. He's got a lot of spoiled-little-rich-girl tricks. Raymond's a bonehead and Randall's a pompous idiot, but Ross is the pick of the bunch."

"I put my foot in it already, when I asked about the gambling."

"What?"

"Randall said I should try and stop him."

"He's gambling my money away?"

"He gambles a lot. But he's got plenty, you know that. The whole family's loaded. What are you worried about?"

"What was the other thing? The other thing you wanted to talk about?"

"About what you'd do if anything happened to me."

"Nothing's going to happen to you."

"What I mean is, there wouldn't be any way you could prove you were Bobby's father. He'd be brought up by the Chases. You knew that before, but now he's actually here. Look." She touched the baby's cheek. It sighed, yawned, opened its eyes, moved its arms and trampled in the air with its feet. She held out a finger. Bobby grabbed it. She made kissing noises at him.

"He's kind of cute," Carter said grudgingly.

"Hold your finger out."

The baby clasped his finger in its hand and chortled.

"It's the way they learn," she said. "They're exercising all the time—with their voices, too. One of those books said that babies make noises even when they're in an empty room, to judge the distances—like echo sounding. Isn't that smart? I've read so many books. I never knew how interesting . . . I mean, we all started like this. We were all this size."

Carter touched the baby's face, its arms, its legs.

"You hold him," Mamie said.

"No."

"Yes. I'm getting tired. They weigh a lot and I don't think these sling things are the best way to lug them around." She handed Bobby over, first showing how to protect his head. Carter held the baby in his arms and looked down. He looked for a long time and turned his head away. "Jesus," he whispered, "what a mess."

She felt secure at last. It was a mess, all right, but now he had to get them out of it. She was sure that somehow he was going to succeed in fixing everything up, and even work it so they'd keep the money, too. "I'll miss him when we go sailing," she said. "Or skiing. They haven't made up their minds yet. I wanted to take him with us, but they all say it's better not to. And then they can get him onto the bottle while I'm drying out."

"What?" Carter said. "I wasn't listening."

"We're going to wean Bobby while he's with the nurse and we're on this vacation."

"Has he made a will?"

"We both did. At the same time we made out all the new insurance papers."

"New? You didn't tell me that."

"It's only the normal thing. Especially if you've just started a family."

"How much are you insured for?"

"Oh, thousands and thousands. The limit."

"Just like Julie."

"But so is he."

"That isn't going to matter, if he's the one pushing you over the railings."

"I don't believe it."

"That's how it happened to her."

"Then they wouldn't try the same way again, would they?"

"People who commit murders usually stick to a pattern."

"Have you ever killed anyone?"

He turned his head again. He said, "If I had to get rid of somebody who was in my way—somebody who deserved it—I wouldn't feel guilty. Would you?"

"Yes. That's how people get caught. They want to talk about it. Because they feel bad."

"I bet some of them feel better afterward. Everybody wants to kill at least one person. Don't you?"

"Of course not."

"Maybe not at the moment. But think back to when you were working in the theater. Nobody you hated?"

"Two people."

"I've got four at the office. And if you could have gotten away with it, wouldn't you have liked to?"

"Just for that moment of destroying them. But afterward,

think what it would do to you. How lonely and miserable you'd feel."

"Not me." He handed Bobby back to her. "You've got to be the one to do it," he said. "It'll be easy for you. They won't suspect you for a minute, the mother of such a cute little baby."

"Did you enjoy your trip?" Katherine asked.

"It was great.The girls all loved him. They cried. He was the only one that didn't. He was so good. Where is everybody?"

The others were out. Katherine asked her to take the baby up to the nursery and then come down to the study to have a cup of coffee and a chat.

Marilyn brought the coffee on one of the big silver trays. She came back with a plate of sandwiches. It still gave Mamie the creeps to have servants bringing things in and taking them out all the time. At the beginning, she'd thought it would be wonderful: gracious living like the advertisements. But what it meant in practice was that you could never be alone. And in her white uniform Marilyn looked more like a nurse than a maid.

Katherine said, "I wanted to talk to you, Rhoda, before we go away. Of course there's time enough—a couple of months. But I always think it's best to settle up as you go along; not to let things slide."

Mamie nodded. She didn't think she was ever going to like her mother-in-law, but she was no longer afraid of her. She could even see that Katherine was a lonely woman. She also knew that she herself had the approval of all the men in the family and that that was what counted with the Chases, even with Katherine.

"I've always been proud of my boys. Raymond and Randall were so good at sports . . ."

Loose-living studs, Mamie thought, *both headed toward the same path their father had taken and the same sauce he was pickled in.*

". . . and now at the bank."

Checking in late in the morning and out early in the afternoon, with a so-called business lunch in between, and playing around with their secretaries, sometimes right in the office.

"And Russell . . ."

Russell, the baby. It didn't show too much; his father had made him join all those games like the others, so he was in pretty good condition physically. But he hadn't escaped his mother.

"He was the really bright one at school. He always had his own ideas about the way things should be. We thought he'd go to the top. But—I do see he was right: he convinced us that the study of nature was just as important. Of course we know it is. It's just that sometimes it seems to me a shame that somebody who has a talent for a thing—that he should have avoided developing it. I expect you know he sometimes plays roulette and twenty-one."

"Yes. He's interested in working out his systems."

"I used to believe so. But it's an odd thing: you can go along believing something for years, and suddenly you know the truth in a flash. We all used to think this sort of gambling fever would come over Ross in waves—he'd go out and lose a lot and then come back and devote himself to the invention of a new set of numbers. I used to think the craving struck him when he was unhappy: that it was an addiction like alcohol."

Everybody had an addiction, Mamie thought. Her father-in-law and the two other sons had liquor, sometimes women; Katherine had her position in the community. And she herself had Carter.

"I wasn't looking at the facts," Katherine said. "The facts are simply that gambling is the quickest way there is of throwing money away. Our family is a banking family and all the men in it, except Russell, work in the bank. He never wanted to—that was all right. But his choice of work didn't stop his feeling against it: guilt, or rebellion, or whatever it is. I don't understand it."

Neither did Mamie. It seemed crazy. Most people would do just about anything for money. Money could change your life. She could certainly understand the excitement of gambling, but only if you were poor. Rich people didn't need to gamble; they had it already.

Katherine said, "He needs someone to take him in hand. Now that you're both parents, it's important for you to think of the future."

"I don't know much about money," Mamie said.

"But perhaps you could speak to him. I think you ought to."

"All right. I will. And maybe you could help me with something."

"About finances?"

"No. It's something I can't ask Ross about. It's about his first wife, Julie."

"Yes?"

"I just want to know about her. I don't have the feeling that something's being kept back from me, or anything—it's just that I can't ask him. What was she like?"

"Very attractive. Intelligent, well read, good background, knew how to dress; perfect manners."

And Carter loved her.

"I didn't mean that," Mamie said. "I want to know what she was like as a person, why Ross married her, whether she was at all like me, or whether she was my opposite."

"Not quite your opposite, but certainly very different. She gave the impression of being always cheerful and efficient, in control. She'd had a very good job, a responsible position in a large firm. She was one of those girls who could be a managing director if she wanted to. Very outgoing, pleasant, put people at their ease."

Mamie could imagine Sal saying, "Miss Vogue"; that was the way they referred to certain people, and clothes, and parts in plays, where all the details were neat and matching and everything looked as if it had been designed by a machine.

"But," she said, "we look alike."

"No, not at all."

"Oh?"

"No. She was tall, above average height. Dark brown hair and—"

"Do you have a photograph?" Mamie said.

"Yes, I think so. Of course. All the wedding pictures, and

from the summer, and that Christmas before the accident."

"Tell me about the accident."

"She just slipped. It was dreadful."

"Was it on snow or on a rock face?"

"I think it must have been a slippery place, maybe ice, or just snow that was packed down."

"Weren't you there?"

"We were all there, except Waverley—he wasn't feeling very well that morning. I was trying to keep up with the boys, and Ross and Julie were behind us. It was a frightful thing. He said he just looked back and she was in the air, falling away. It took him a long time to get over it."

"Could I see the pictures?" Mamie asked.

Katherine led the way upstairs to her room. She brought out a pile of photograph albums, found the one she wanted and took it over to the window seat.

Mamie sat down too. She held half the large album while Katherine turned the pages and told off the names and talked about the places. There were lots of pictures of Julie: tall, self-confident, with the dark hair and the fashion-model look.

"Why did you think," Katherine asked, "that you looked alike?"

"It was something Carter Mathews said that time he was here. Maybe he meant it in some other way."

"Such a good-looking boy. But unreliable."

"Um."

"And quite notorious with women, always has at least three or four on a string at the same time."

"Yes," Mamie mumbled, "I kind of got that impression about him."

She wore the comedy mask on a thin silver chain around her neck. The morning after she'd come back from seeing Carter she was leaning down and forward near a chair Russell was sitting in, and he asked her, "Is there only one of those masks? I thought the other one was right behind the—"

"No," she said, "there's only one. The comedy one."

"You don't like tragedy?"

"I lost the other one."

"I suppose it wouldn't be too hard to replace it."

"I don't want to. I like it the way it is, now. I'm used to it like this."

"I don't mind tragedy. It shows the character."

Thinking of her mother, she said, "Unless there's too much of it. Then people start to lose their personality. They go dead."

"I don't call that tragedy."

"What do you call it?"

"Just bad luck."

"Uh-huh. There's a lot of it around."

"But not for us," he said, smiling fatuously at her. She made him knock on wood. She ran the mask back and forth on its chain until it zinged.

He said, "My old teacher at the institute would get a kick out of that. The one time I got away from home—and he spent half the time telling me about America. He was always saying that Americans sentimentalized and falsified everything in order to make life more comfortable. No more tragedy, only fun. And the idealists had the concept of worthy effort—that was their form of fun."

"Well, if you could get rid of the bad parts, wouldn't you?"

"You get rid of them by living through them."

Mamie laughed. "Sure," she said.

"You don't think so?"

"I don't know. All I know is what we used to say in the profession: comedy ends in marriage, tragedy ends in death."

"You could take that both ways. Are you saying that once you're married, the comedy's over?"

"No, it's—"

"And once you're dead, the tragedy's over?"

"Once you're dead, everything's over."

"You believe that?"

"All I said was: that's the way they end."

"Or it could mean intent—that the purpose of comedy is marriage. And the purpose of tragedy—"

"I'm getting mixed up now," she said. She was also getting bored. He never teased her or laughed at her like Carter; he genuinely didn't think she was dumb. And she was gratified by the way he took her opinions so seriously; but sometimes he could go on and on until she wanted to jump up and start kicking the furniture. Her mother had said: *Marry a rich man and you'll never have to worry.* But it wasn't enough, even though her position had changed. When she was with Russell, she was in control. When she was with Carter, he was the one who had the power, because she was the one who loved. She was tied to both men without really knowing either of them. And she had two lives that she couldn't live right. Every minute she had to watch her step, to try to remember what she was supposed to be doing.

Russell had read a lot of plays and he could talk about them, but he didn't like going out much. She thought he'd rather stick with the plays in books. He even said once that the theater wasn't like real life. Of course it wasn't, she'd said, any more than a painted portrait was a real face. They were both pictures. And there were good pictures or bad pictures—that was the only important question. He said something about artificiality. She didn't know where to begin on that argument. The house she lived in, her marriage, her whole life was artificial.

He'd go to movies. Occasionally he'd suggest going out for a meal and a film, but that was for her sake. He didn't find pleasure in the town; he preferred to see movies on television. What he really loved was his job. He also liked, and enjoyed playing with, and began to love, Bobby. When Mamie watched the two of them laughing and making faces at each other, she became fond of Russell and was happy in his company. At those moments she almost believed she belonged to him. And she started to get used to being married, and to think of it as normal.

He tried to tell her about biology—how large the scope of it was, and what it could explain. She listened as if fascinated. Sometimes, in fact, she found herself becoming interested, but usually it was because she thought that Carter would like to hear it.

"It's beyond all other things," Russell told her. "It's the

basis. Whatever the future holds, there are millions of years behind us, and they're part of us: we're the product of them. All our instincts, everything."

"Our thoughts?" she asked.

"Maybe not. But our dreams, certainly. They're the same as they always were. What kind of dreams do you have?"

"Oh, I don't know. Nice ones. And the bad ones. I guess being chased, or caught in a fire, or drowning or something. But that was only—I used to have horrible nightmares when I was little. Everybody does, don't they? And then I grew out of it. What kind of dreams do you have?"

"I have one that repeats," he said. "I'm standing alone in a high place. It's getting dark, there's someone behind me I can't see. And I'm afraid to turn around."

"And that's all? That's the whole thing?"

"That's enough. It's very creepy and it usually wakes me up in a sweat. You'll see. Or maybe they'll stop, now that I've got you with me."

"That would be nice," she said.

"Cured by a woman's love. If comedy ends in marriage, where does it begin?"

"Laughing. Jokes."

"And tragedy?"

"What?" She'd forgotten where they'd left the conversation.

"Tragedy begins at home," he said.

"That's charity, Ross."

"Oh, yes. Charity."

She thought he might have meant to imply something about her, but he started almost immediately to look through a book he had with him; he wanted to show her a picture. He spoke of trained, scientific observation; about animals, birds and insects. "You see these creatures," he said, "and they're capable of astonishing things—amazing. We call it instinct, but they're so inspired, they seem to know about cause and effect. And look here: the way the color of the skin and fur and feathers has evolved to suit the climate and the habitat. It all seems to be so much more intelligent than ordinary thought. And simpler."

*   *   *

She asked Russell to take her out for a drive in the country. It was like arranging a meeting with Carter. She wanted to talk to him outside the house.

She said, "There's something I've got to ask you. You remember, Randall told me to tell you about gambling? Well, now your mother's leaning on me. I just wanted to know what's behind it."

"When I was in high school and made my big decision to go into biology, you should have seen all the tricks they tried. They actually sent me to a doctor. They'd have sent me to a psychiatrist except that it would have ruined my career to have that on my record."

"Why?"

"Well, who goes to psychiatrists? Crazy people—right? You can be as crazy as you like, but once you've seen a psychiatrist, it's official. Everybody knows it and they won't hire you, not even in a bank. In a bank what you should be worrying about is theft and embezzlement."

"And gambling?"

"We call it investment. You want to know why they're in such a sweat? Because if I sold my shares on the open market, the family would drop from a sixty percent majority share-holder down to forty-eight percent. So, if the other fifty-two percent wanted to vote in a block, they could start kicking people off the board. That kind of thing."

"Would you?"

"I might. Or I might give them the choice of buying me out at a slightly higher price. That's what people usually do."

"You seem to get along OK with them."

"Sure."

"It would just about kill your mother, wouldn't it? And your father?"

"They feel that way about everything. It might be good for the bank to have a couple of new people giving orders. Why not?"

"She said a peculiar thing, too. She said you were trying to throw your money away, and gambling was the quickest way of doing it."

"I hadn't thought of that. Was that all you wanted to talk about?"

"Yes. I don't know what to do when they say, 'You tell Russell this,' or 'Tell him that.' I mean, I can't just say, 'Tell him yourself,' can I?"

"Try it. See what happens. Or—no, it's better if you don't; this way, I can find out what's on their minds."

"Think of myself as a soldier operating in enemy territory? Or as an actress playing a part?"

"That's right."

"Why do they assume I won't pass everything on to you?"

"They probably can't believe we talk together like other married couples."

"Why not?"

"I don't know."

"Is it something about me?"

"Or me. I'm the one they always had trouble with. I won't fit in. There are a lot of wives who sit and listen to other people's good advice and they start to think to themselves that maybe their husband really does need to be changed around; so they don't say anything to him, they just start heckling him the way the others told them to."

Julie did that, Mamie thought.

Carter was waiting for her in the cocktail lounge. She missed her step as she came up to him and he caught her quickly. She'd forgotten how strong he was; it was like the kind of sudden tackle you might see in a football game. He kissed her cheek.

"That all I get?" she asked.

"You've been drinking. You aren't supposed to drink, are you?"

"I'm all dried out now. I can have a drink or two."

"You've had so many, you can't walk straight."

"Two drinks, that's all. I'm fine. It's so fucking dark in here, like all these places. Your favorite word, for my favorite activity. Want to hit me? Want me to say it a little louder?"

"I think we'd better go someplace less public."

"Fine by me. I'd like a drink first."

"OK. One." He went to the bar and brought her back a gin and tonic. "All right?" he said, as he put the glass down in front of her.

"Sure. Same likes, same dislikes. Here's to our wonderful future."

"I thought you were going to bring the baby."

"To a place like this?"

"I thought we'd go somewhere else. We could have gone to my place."

"I'm not supposed to be seen there, am I?"

"Drink that up. We've got to talk. What's gotten into you all of a sudden?"

"I've been seeing some very interesting photographs."

"Of me?"

"Maybe. Which ones did you have in mind?"

"Well, I did a lot of crazy things when I was around college age. I even made a porno movie with a few friends."

"Oh-ho?"

"We were all stoned, but we made a lot of money out of it."

"Is that a fact? I expect you're sorry about it now."

"Of course not. What's a picture? They could cover the front page with pictures of me doing it with an elephant. I wouldn't mind."

"Jesus, I'd die."

"I still think it's funny. I think it's even funnier that some of those guys are busting themselves trying to get the prints back. But you're right; the girls felt differently. They had a great time going along with everything until later. And then all of them—every single one—started to freak out about it: the idea that somebody they knew might see it. Or that lots of people could see it, who'd never met them, and somebody might spot them on the street or in a store or waiting for an elevator someday and say, 'I've seen you before, and guess where?' "

"That's terrible. I think that's awful, Carter."

"It had a pretty bad effect on them. I don't understand it. If they felt that way, why did they join in? What the hell?"

"Maybe after they fell in love and got married; they could be afraid of being blackmailed. They wouldn't want their husbands to know. You don't want people you love to know things about you that aren't nice."

He threw down the book of matches he'd been playing with. All the matches were splayed and ripped; the cover was almost shredded. She couldn't make out his expression, even though her eyes had adjusted to the dim light. It might have been the look of a man who blackmailed women.

"Let's go to my place," he said.

It was the first time they'd been together since shortly after her marriage. He told her she was more beautiful than before the baby; she was more fun. They went out once for a meal and came back again. She stayed most of the night. She could have stayed right through till morning and for the whole of the day, but she needed alibis just in case: the hotel bills, the theater ticket stubs, and so on. As he walked her up to the hotel doorway, he said, "Better than the photographs?"

"They weren't of you. They were of your cousin Julie. The one who looks just like me, remember?"

"Here," he said, touching the side of her face. "That's what I saw. It seems a lot less pronounced now that I know you."

"Come on, Carter. We're as different as black and white."

"Black and white can look very similar. I told you: resemblance doesn't depend on that. Especially in a photograph."

"Funny how you thought it had to be pictures of you."

"It's probably just as well I told you. Things like that have a habit of popping up when you don't expect them. The horselaugh out of the past."

"I brought you some pictures, too," she said. "I'll show you tomorrow."

The next day, when they were in bed together, she reached over to the night table for her handbag, opened it and brought out a large envelope full of photographs of the baby. She began to hand them to him one by one.

"Nice," he told her. "Look at us. All three of us here, and

not a stitch on. Next time you come, bring him with you. I'm tired of being so careful."

"It isn't worth taking the chance. You know what could happen legally."

"Did they tell you where you're going on the vacation?"

"Some tiny little place in Switzerland. Or maybe it was Austria." She told him the name.

"That's the same place," he said. "It's where they pushed her over the side."

"No, it isn't. The name under the photographs is different."

"It's the same area, right down the valley."

"But not the same place. Not the same village. Is it?"

"Not exactly. It's right near it."

"But not the same. That's what you said at first, wasn't it?"

"It doesn't sound good to me. Maybe the bank is on the rocks again, or Russell's in debt. You're insured right up to your ears."

"So is he. It's the usual thing."

"Who does your will leave everything to?"

"The new one leaves it to Bobby. Russell gets the interest till he's grown up."

"And if Bobby dies?"

"Bobby?"

"Babies can get sick and die before you even realize anything's wrong. We should have gone through all this before."

"But we did. We've been over and over everything. It goes to Russell. How could I leave it to you? I couldn't."

"You could go to another lawyer and make a second will. And that's what I think you'd better do."

She got out of bed and began to put on her clothes. She went into the bathroom, then to the kitchen. Carter came in after her and handed her a coffee cup. He poured out some coffee for her, and some for himself.

He said, "That's a horrible dress."

"Russell likes it. He chose it himself. It's better than just that towel." She started to get annoyed. She said, "Want to hear what else he likes?"

"I think maybe it should have something spilled on it."

All at once she was furious. She turned around, put her cup down on the edge of the sink and said that before the baby was born she gave Russell excuses for not making love, but that afterward they'd started to, the way they should have from the beginning, and now they were like any other married couple: they did it all the time; and it was so good with him—yes, honestly—because he was affectionate and made her feel happy.

Carter laughed. He sat down at the table.

She said, "I'll call you up when we get back from skiing."

"I'll be reading the obituary columns, looking for Russell."

"Let's drop it. Please. You're wearing me out."

"No stamina. You were ready to go through with it."

"I was never ready to kill anybody. Never. I can't even remember why you told me I had to get married to him. It's always one story on top of another."

He said, "If you don't, he'll get you for the insurance money."

She didn't believe it. She started to pace up and down. She said, "We're always talking about killing. It's driving me nuts."

"If you're the one that does it, they won't suspect anything."

"I don't have to do a thing. No. I can do just nothing and I can have you both. You can tell him what you like. I'll say you're trying to blackmail me. I'll start doing what you do. I don't care. You can go to hell."

He put his elbows on the table, his hands over his ears, and moaned.

She heard herself panting in the stillness. He looked terrible. He started to whisper to himself. "They always said it would happen to me. My mother used to warn me: *You'll end up like your father.*"

"What happened to your father?" They were both whispering now.

"One day he just snapped. He killed seven people with an ax."

Her heartbeat gave a thump and rushed upward. She came

forward slowly. She put her arms around him. "It's all right," she said gently.

He lifted his face, took his elbows off the table and suddenly pulled her down into the chair with him. "You fell for it?" he asked. He picked up his cup and said, "This is cold." He poured coffee all over her dress.

They rolled onto the floor, fighting and laughing. He started to tickle her. He got her to unsay everything she'd claimed about her married life, to tell him she couldn't live without him, to say she never stopped thinking about him, and to tell him she wanted more.

"You're so mean to me," she sighed. "Honest to God."

He said, "I'm not mean. I'm just violent. I thought you liked it."

"We've got everything we want," she told him. "We had everything all along—enough money, too. Lots of people in the world don't even get enough to eat every day."

"The hell with them. They should get up off their knees and start hitting back. They deserve all they get."

"I should never have married him."

"Fur coats, diamonds? What's that ring you've got on right now? And that car you told me about?"

"I can get by without any of it. Nothing wrong with buses. I can take the subway. I can walk. All I want is you and Bobby."

"We wouldn't even be able to afford the bus after a while. I'm leaving my job."

"Why?'"

"Because I'm not going to need it anymore."

"You see? None of it makes sense. If you were really planning to do anything, that would look bad."

"I can't help it. I can't take it anymore."

"And another thing: they all talk about an accident, but if she just fell, how come you got a suicide note?"

"I've never understood that. All I can think of is that they'd planned to do it a little later in some other way that wasn't going to look so natural. I just don't know."

He waited in the car outside her hotel and then drove her to the airport. They sat in the parking lot until it was time. "Remember," he said. "Let me know what happens. At the number I gave you."

"I'll try. I get so mixed up about all the special words."

"Just keep calm: don't get flustered. I'm going to have to know everything now. I'll be coming with you."

"I'm not doing it. I told you. And you aren't, either."

"I'm just going, to try to keep you alive. Even if you start out assuming they didn't do it, why would they want to go back there? Why would innocent people act like that?"

She promised to tell him everything. They kissed goodbye. Then she said, "You never did tell me about your father, or the rest of your family."

"Some other time."

"We've still got a few minutes."

"Would it surprise you very much to know that Waverley Chase is my father? My real father?"

"Yes, it would. Is he?"

"Maybe." He kissed her again.

"Carter," she said, "I can't put up with any more of this fooling."

He opened the door, got out, and started to walk around to her side. She was out of the car before he came up to her.

"Is he?" she asked.

"You think about it on the way back."

"Tell me now, Carter, or I'm going to let that plane go without me."

"OK, OK. As far as I know, that whiskey-sodden old windbag could only be the father of those three jerks you're living with. Satisfied?"

"Was there something wrong with your father?"

"Why?"

"Because you won't tell me about him."

"Nothing to tell, about either of them. Just ordinary people."

"But you aren't ordinary."

"I was adopted."

They reached the departure lounge before she turned to him and said, "Then Julie wasn't your real cousin?"

"She was adopted, too."

"I don't believe it."

He laughed.

"Are you adopted?" she hissed at him. "I'm not getting on the plane until you tell me. Are you?"

"We are boarding at this time," a stewardess said almost in her ear. She backed toward the exit, still asking, "Are you?"

He shook his head.

She wanted to sleep on the flight, but couldn't. She kept thinking about heredity and everything she'd read in the books and magazines. Such a sweet baby, always laughing, couldn't have inherited anything bad. But Carter laughed a lot, too. And maybe his father had been laughing when he'd had the ax in his hand; except—there hadn't been any ax. It was made up. She was so confused that each time she thought she'd figured something out, she had to accept a new contradiction. A few days later, she thought: If Carter kept telling her Julie was his favorite cousin, that must mean he had more than one. Who were the other ones?

The only person she could think of asking was her husband. She told him that when she'd been in town seeing her friends backstage, she'd heard about another girl, who was going around with Carter and wasn't very happy.

"What do you know about him?" she asked.

"Not as much as you," he said. "You were going out with him. In fact, you were sleeping with him, weren't you?"

His tone was light but nasty. She hadn't expected that he'd give the affair a thought. She said penitently, "Just at the beginning, yes. It was before I met you. And anyway, I never knew where I was with him. That's why I want to find out. He was always so secretive about himself."

"I can tell you what he was like in school and college: in on every scheme you could name, even some that were a little risky. And getting away with everything. And a big reputation with the girls, which you know about."

"He kept talking about his cousin all the time. About Julie. He said she was his favorite cousin. I just wondered—who were the others? His other cousins."

"Oh. That's us. Didn't he tell you? We're cousins, too. What did he say when he brought you here?"

"That Waverley and Katherine had been his parents' best friends. Why would he lie?"

"Why would he do anything? That's the way he is. None of us liked him. Since we've grown up, we haven't seen much of him. Once a year, maybe, or less."

"So it was a big surprise when he showed up with me that time?"

"He wanted to talk with Father about his shares in the bank."

"Carter's shares?"

"That kind of thing. We don't see him for just family feeling. My parents don't mind him. And you thought he was all right."

"I still think so, but I never got the feeling I really knew him."

"Sometimes it's hard to tell with people," he said. "They put on an act."

"You mean me?"

"Of course not. With you, I can always tell."

"Oh?"

"Always," he said.

She'd never been to another country. She didn't like the idea. Katherine, who delighted in traveling and holidays, was considerate to her and patted her arm as they sat in the airport bar. "You'll love it when we get there," she said. "I know you will. Just relax and have a good time."

Waverley bought her a good stiff drink. He had one himself. She became sentimental and frightened when she thought about leaving Bobby. She whimpered into her drink, "I don't think it's right for such a little baby to be away from its mother for such a long time."

"Oh, you can count on Evie," Katherine told her. "She's got all the right references. She'll have him in a fixed routine before you know it. When we get back, you'll find him doing everything like clockwork. All our friends say she's a marvel at discipline."

She couldn't say what she thought. The moment the brisk and self-important Evie had marched across the threshold, Mamie had detested her. There was nothing she could do about it. The choice wasn't hers; perhaps it never would be. She wouldn't have known how to go about hiring someone, or which nurse to pick. She wouldn't have wanted to choose anyone in the first place.

They stepped into the plane, buckled themselves in, took off. They were on a night flight. She hugged the airline pillow to her. She hated the plane, she hated Russell. She hated everything and she couldn't sleep.

"Isn't this better?" Katherine asked.

Mamie looked around at the blue sky, the white snow-fields, the tiny villages down below. The world was bright and sparkling. "It's all like toys," she said.

They were escorted into their hotel. Uniformed bellboys carried their bags, opened the doors. She hadn't imagined the mountains would be equipped with anything so luxurious. She'd had a vague picture in her mind of a lot of people in leather shorts.

Carter was staying in the neighboring valley. They were to meet the next day. She had the excuse of not knowing how to ski, so she was going to be down at the beginners' practice area, taking lessons while the others were out on the higher slopes or traveling up and down by the chair lifts and the cable car.

Raymond had spent all the first morning showing her how the different lifts worked. She'd been strapped into one mechanical device after another. The most difficult had been the slow one, where you hung on by your arms and had to keep your skis from moving apart as you were pulled along over the ground. But the most terrifying had been the one where you retained the heavy skis, sat on the T-bar, and were lifted so high above the ground that you could look down: on the tops of trees that grew in icy gorges miles below. She'd been so afraid that she hadn't dared to call out anything to Raymond, who was sitting in the seat ahead of her. He'd remained untroubled by the height, and kept turning around to talk. The skis had pulled downward. She'd thought she could keep her leg muscles fixed but if her hands and arms began to shake, that would be the end. The fir trees underneath their path were the biggest she had ever seen and their surrounding landscape looked as forbidding as a scene out of prehistoric times. Raymond twisted his head around and smiled. When they were free of the tow she told him, "I never want to go on that one again. I was afraid I was going to fall out, or maybe even jump out."

"Do heights make you dizzy?"

"I don't know. I've never been on anything like that before."

"I was just thinking—when we take the walk over the pass together; I guess Ross can take care of you."

She wasn't sure she'd be going on any walk. She felt stiff all over. She passed the greater part of that first afternoon picking herself up off the ground and trying to keep the skis from sliding in opposite directions. In the end she gave up and went to sit on the observation porch and drink cocoa while she watched the skaters. And she rehearsed what she was going to say to Carter.

Carter's village was unspoiled compared with the complex of big hotels, restaurants, discotheques and casinos higher up the mountainside. It was still a real village, with a church, and local people who didn't speak English. The children slid down the steep main street on sleds, the grown-ups were climbing or leaning from ladders propped against a group of mammoth snow statues that they were building. The statues portrayed characters and stories from the Bible. The three kings were finished already, while work went on around the ox, the ass, and—the most important—the Virgin holding her child in her arms. The tallest figures stood higher than the housetops nearby; and they seemed to have been shaped according to some principle handed down through the generations, since all had approximately the same look, or style. They reminded

Mamie of the faces on playing cards, or of chessmen, or certain kinds of puppets.

"There's a lot less neon down here," Carter said. "See all this authentic culture? You don't get that up in the fleshpots."

"What do you do in the evenings?"

"There's a tavern. And the pensions serve beer and liquor."

"No dancing?"

"Next village."

"But I guess it costs a lot anyway. How can you afford to be here at all?"

"I sold some stuff. And I borrowed some." He pulled her along by the hand, up a set of steps cut into the snow. "Come look at the church," he said.

"What for?"

"Listen."

They stopped outside the doorway and waited while two men moved what looked like part of a wardrobe into the building. Mamie could hear music coming from somewhere ahead of them.

She stepped forward, through the thick curtains and into the church. Carter followed.

He put his arm around her, led her into a pew, and began to whisper in her ear. "They practice every morning and afternoon. I think it's just the local school kids, but maybe they're from the whole area. Pretty good, aren't they?"

She looked around at the carved wood, the painted plaster lilies and angels, and at the schoolchildren playing their fiddles and flutes. It was the only nice church she'd ever been in. She'd have liked to stay all day.

He took her to a different village in order to talk. They sat in the corner of a dining room that belonged to a small hotel. For an hour and a half they talked. He drank three beers, she had four cups of coffee. He wanted her to kill Russell. She said, "Don't be ridiculous." He threatened to go to the Chase family with lies, or even with the truth; he started to make her laugh. He told her stories.

She could see what he was doing; she'd watched it on the stage so many times when they'd played farce, but she'd always gotten it wrong herself because she couldn't keep the

tempo—that was what it depended on: his timing was
perfect. He knew how to slow you down and when to
accelerate, to make you shape your timing to his. He made
you believe from moment to moment that it was all real, that
he was telling the truth, that the way he'd put it was right,
and that he loved you best.

"No," she said. "I'll get a divorce."

"I know that bastard. He'll keep the kid."

"They wouldn't allow that."

"They'd prove you were an unfit mother. An unwholesome
moral influence. Undereducated, no money of your own, no
background."

"They can't. The law wouldn't let them."

"Oh, a few dollars in the right places. I told you, I know
how these things work."

"Don't," she said.

"It's true."

"They wouldn't let him. You couldn't blame him for
trying, I guess. He'd have a right to try. He really does love
Bobby."

"Rights over my kid? Mine?" He sounded just the way he'd
sounded when he talked about all the money that was
supposed to be his.

"I liked that church," she said. "The last time I was in
church was when I had a headache. I just wanted to sit down
and rest." She told him about the preacher who believed
she'd come into his church to commune with God. Carter was
highly amused. And, as always, she felt inordinately pleased
at having been able to entertain him. But when she thought
back, she remembered that sitting in the church that time
hadn't been so funny.

He raised his glass of beer. He said, "That's what I love
about you, Rhoda. You make me laugh."

"I guess not many people go into churches at those
in-between times unless it's a kind of emergency."

"Maybe he thought you were a fallen woman."

"Especially young people. Church wouldn't be the first
place any young person thinks of. It was fun to see all those
school kids playing their music."

"Are you thinking of going religious on me all of a sudden?"

"I never told you much about the birth, did I? You aren't interested in things like that. There was one point where I was having a pretty bad time. I was sure I was going to die. I really was. I couldn't kill anybody, Carter."

"We'll see."

"No. I couldn't."

"We'll talk about it tomorrow," he said.

"I can't keep talking about things. I'm worn out."

"You look all right. All this healthy air. How do you like this part of the world?"

"Oh, it's very—well, it's nice, of course. But it's so different."

"It looks beautiful, doesn't it?"

"Yes."

"So white, so clean. But the cold can be without pity. I remember reading about those mountaineering teams when I was growing up; all the famous ones—Everest, and everything. There was one story I remember, about going up the Eiger: one guy was left out there for a long time, and when they got to him, all he could say was, "Cold, hungry." He'd already eaten up the leather straps on everything he owned and he'd started to eat his lips."

"Don't tell me. I hate that kind of thing."

"I love it. Stories like that tell you what people are really like."

"That's only what they're like when awful things happen."

"They happen all the time. You can't say people only behave that way in extremity. All life is extremity. What about right at the beginning of that climb—that man's decision to set out in the first place? Was that a crazy idea?"

She thought about the snow outside and said, "Yes, of course it was."

"Well, I can see myself doing the same thing."

"So can I."

"You'd never get past the ski lift."

"So can I see you," she said. "I can see you doing the same thing. I wouldn't want to."

They walked out into the cold again. A girl coming toward them smiled knowingly at Carter and said, "Hi, there." He said, "Hi," and kept going.

"Who's that?" Mamie asked. She was angry for not being able to stop herself saying anything. What would he tell her, anyway? Just the usual.

"Oh," he said, "somebody. I don't know. A snow bunny."

The girl had been wearing a red fox jacket. A girl like that would have plenty of money. And she hadn't looked too obvious, either. She looked born rich: she'd have come to the ski resort as a victim, not a predator. With so many women like that around, Carter wouldn't have to kill for money; he really could marry it. He'd reminded her before that he was still free.

She could sense him preparing to frighten her with the possibility. She'd be too tired to rise to it at the moment, but on another occasion, it might work.

When they passed by the church and the snow statues, it was already getting dark. There were lights on in front of the inns and hotels. People called to each other, their voices carrying clearly in the cold, pure air. The giant snow figures glowed with their own whiteness; even in the twilight people were still working on them. He pulled her into an alley between two houses, to kiss her before she went back up the mountain.

She arrived at the hotel in plenty of time to take a shower before dinner. Russell talked to her from the other side of the door. He said, "Mother doesn't want me in the casino. It's such a bore to be told the same thing over and over."

"Well, she worries about you," Mamie answered. "She doesn't understand why you'd want to keep doing it when you always lose. Like she said: you're throwing it away."

"Why don't you try to stop me?"

"I'm not your mother," she said. "Besides, you wouldn't quit until you wanted to, would you?" She hung up her bathrobe and put on a slip.

He sat on the stool in front of the dressing table until she came over and moved next to him. He got up, crossed to the windows and stood there, fingering the drawn curtains. He

said, "I saw Carter down in one of the villages this morning.
Were you with him today?"

She said yes without turning her head. She heard his feet
moving. He came into sight in the mirror. He sat down on the
bed.

He asked, "Are you still sleeping with him?"

"No," she said quickly, "I told you all about that."

"Oh, I know what you told me."

"Well, it's true."

"That day you took the baby to town," he said, "I followed
you. That's another good thing about a job like mine. But I
took a plane. It was easy. You went to the theater. Yes. To the
department store. And then you met him in the park. That's
when I knew: when I saw him playing with the baby. It's his
child, isn't it?"

She put her head down in front of the mirror. For months
she'd expected him to say something and she'd gone over her
answer—lots of different possible answers; and now she
could barely get the sound out. She sobbed and said no,
Bobby was his child, but Carter wouldn't let her alone and
kept threatening to tell lies about her, and in fact that was just
what he'd said he was going to do: "He said he'd even go tell
you our baby was actually his, unless I did what he wanted."
She got up from the stool, fell toward the bed and threw
herself at him, protesting. She wept noisily, happy to let go.
It was making her less afraid. And it dismayed him. Carter
was unmoved by tears, but Russell couldn't deal with them.

"Stop, please," he said. "Don't cry like that."

"But you wouldn't believe him, would you?"

"OK, I know all about Carter. We've been through that. He
was after Julie's money."

"He said he loved her."

"Love? Carter doesn't work that way."

She sniffed and stopped crying. She said, "Do you think
we ought to get a divorce?"

"Of course not. Why?"

"If you're suspecting things like that, I don't know. You
can't love me much."

He put a finger on the side of her jaw and turned her face

toward him, saying, "You know, in certain lights you look just like her. Like my first wife. You're such different types, but it's there."

"Do you think about her a lot?"

"No. But here in the mountains, I guess it can't help but be on our minds."

"It must have been terrible," she said. "I've wanted to talk to you about it before, but I thought it would bring back painful memories."

"Yes, it was," he said. "Terrible." He drew in his breath and added, "She was a real bitch. Always telling me what to do. Always right about everything. Always knew best."

Late in the night she woke up and felt scared. The room was hot and completely dark. She told herself that the dressing table was in front, the yellow curtains to the left, the bathroom at the right. She grew more and more afraid.

She thought Carter was lying to her, but she loved him. She didn't know anything about Russell any longer and suddenly wondered if he liked her at all.

He liked biology. He liked the subject. She wasn't sure how much he liked people. He was polite, which made it harder to tell. His own mother wasn't sure how he felt.

In spite of all the lies Carter told, maybe it really was possible that Russell had pushed his first wife to her death. If there were some way of knowing for certain whether Russell believed that Bobby wasn't his—then, Mamie thought, she'd feel safer.

She wanted to see Carter right away, but he was out. She took her skiing lesson on the slope, went back to the hotel for lunch and played cards with Katherine, Waverley and an old woman they'd run into, who was a friend they hadn't seen for many years.

During one hand when she was dummy, Mamie was called to the telephone. It was Carter, saying that he'd found the note she'd left and that they could meet late in the afternoon.

There was to be a hockey game in one of the valleys that night. Randall and Raymond were planning to go to it, but Russell had said he wanted to see the movie the hotel was showing. Mamie told Katherine that she had to pick up a sweater she'd left down at the ski lodge: she'd go get it, have something to eat, and meet the boys later at the hockey game.

"I'd like to get down there early and watch them working on the snow statues while it's still light," she explained. "I can get a snack. I'm already eating too much."

No one questioned her about anything. She'd left her partner, the little old lady, to play out a small slam doubled and redoubled; that was a lot more important than the fact that she was going to spend an evening away from her husband and have dinner alone. No one, except perhaps Russell, would notice her absence. And he proably wouldn't, either. He'd be thinking about going to the casino.

People were crowding together in the village. She and Carter were swept along down the streets with the others heading for the game.

They passed an inn where a woman stood with her back to them. Mamie thought for a moment that she looked just like her mother; and then the woman turned around. She still looked like her mother, but younger. And Mamie thought: *That's what she must have been like before I ever saw her.*

"What's wrong?" Carter asked. He had his arm around her. She said she was fine.

It was almost dark. The lights were already on in the houses. As soon as they started on the road up the hill to the stadium, they had the snow and starlight to see by, nothing else. She was puffing by the time they reached the stands of the open arena. The darkening air was deep and freezing.

Carter bought some sausages and beer. They ate and drank as the seats filled up around them. Mamie kept watch for Randall and Raymond. She noticed that she appeared to be the only woman there, although it was hard to tell when everyone was so bundled up. Nobody near her seemed to be speaking English.

"Can you see Randall?" she asked. "Or Ray?"

"We're fine," Carter said. "Now tell me. You're going on the big walk tomorrow, right?"

She said yes, and told him the times and where they planned to start, where they'd end up: at the inn on top of the mountain.

Then she told him what Russell had said about seeing them in the park that day in town.

"Right," Carter said. "That's it. There's no sense in going on with any of it now."

"That's what I think. We go to him together and ask for a divorce."

"And he keeps the kid and the money, too. Nope. You start off on that walk, and make sure you two are the last ones—which you'll be, anyhow, because he's going to do to you just what he did to her. Oh yes, he is."

"I'm not doing anything."

"I'll do it," he said. "I should have known I'd have to. You'd just mess it up."

She felt the same sensation that had come over her on the open ski lift: of steep, quick falling before the fall should begin.

She reached over and put a hand on his knee. She leaned against him. "I don't want—" she said.

"It's all right. We won't talk about it again. Leave it to me."

She tried to say she didn't want it to happen, she didn't want to be there, in a foreign country, surrounded by strangers, and talking about murder. She only wanted to be with him, and get their baby back, and forget everything else.

She stayed clinging to him as the cold grew excruciating. Her feet froze. She couldn't even get the feeling going by stamping up and down on the wood planks. Despite the low temperature the smell of garlic and red wine was overpowering.

The players came skating out onto the ice; red and black jerseys, faces livid under the lights. Up above, in the open air, you could see the stars.

The game began. It looked rough: the teams seemed to hate each other.

"Who are they?" she asked.

"The local boys against somebody—I think it's Vienna." She couldn't follow the action. Men on the ice were shouting at each other and also being yelled at from the stands. A fight broke out. When another commotion started among the spectators down near the ice, she said, "Do you want to stay till it's over? I'm frozen," and they left.

She almost fell to her knees on the walk to the cable car. He whispered, "Remember tomorrow," as she got in. She was numb with the cold and too tired to answer.

She woke late at night. Someone was knocking at the door. She got up and went to answer it. Her mother stood in the doorway with a baby in her arms: she said, "Help me." And she started to tell Mamie that there were people chasing her—she was in danger and needed someplace to hide. But Mamie was afraid and said she couldn't let her in. She closed the door. She woke up.

Later she remembered the baby her mother had been holding. The baby must have been herself. It must have been, because she'd been her mother's only child.

"If you come with me," Katherine said, "we can set the pace."

"You set it too slow," Randall complained.

"You go on ahead with Father," Russell told Katherine. "In case he needs you. Let Ray and Randy try to beat each other to the top. I'll keep Rhoda company."

The sun came out. It was a wonderful day. They didn't have to exert themselves much at all on the earlier part of the climb, but Mamie tried to go slowly anyway.

"Are you sure your father's going to be all right?" she asked.

"He's in better shape than any of us. A walking advertisement for the health-giving properties of bourbon. Mother's OK, too."

"Oh, I know that. She does all those exercises."

They came to a bend and saw that far above them two other walking parties were starting out from higher lookout posts. Russell said, "This is the last point where you can turn around and look up like this. All the other places are set in. You see the second and third, but there are five more after that: the dangerous ones. The view is incredible—you look right down into crevasses. You'll see. It's like something out of the Ice Age."

"When do you want to eat our sandwiches?"

"We can do that at the next stop. There's a picnic place and a kind of lavatory."

The next lap was a good deal harder. She kept plodding forward without thinking. She could tell already that she was too tired, and that she was going to be stiff and sore for days afterward.

The four others were waiting for them, but had started to eat. Waverley scanned the valley through his field glasses. He broke off to take a swig from a canteen he had with him. "Want to look?" he said.

Mamie lifted the binoculars to her face. It was like seeing into another planet, like being at the movies. Everyone was unaware of the eyes watching from above.

"But it's even more surprising without them," she said. "Everything is so little. I can't believe we've gotten this high up, so quickly."

"There's a lot more, and a lot wilder, beyond this," Russell told her. "But you can't see it from here."

She unpacked her knapsack and started to eat. She was beginning to feel better. Katherine asked assertively whether it wasn't exhilarating up on top of the world. Mamie said yes, definitely.

She wished that she could take the past two years, except for the baby, out of her life and start again. Here, all in brightness, with light bouncing off the blank slopes, she could feel something approaching: it was like the moment before the curtain came down at the theater. Whatever it was, it might fall over her past and cover it forever; and perhaps her future, too.

"It looks like a long way to the end," she said.

Russell stretched out his arm across the picnic table and took her hand in a strong grip. He said, "Rest here awhile longer. I'll stay with you." He smiled. The sun shone on his teeth, his hair, his tinted glasses, through which she could see his eyes. He looked very healthy. He looked as if he were enjoying himself. She nodded and said, "All right."

The others left. She divided the coffee from the thermos bottle between her plastic cup and his.

"How was the casino?" she asked.

"Fine. I lost twelve thousand dollars. How was the whatever-it-was?"

"Hockey game. There were fights, so I came home early. I couldn't even find Randy and Ray."

"Next year," he said, "I think I'll choose a warmer climate." He looked at the view, not at her.

She swallowed. She could believe in anything now. She wasn't afraid, as she had been in the darkness of the hotel bedroom, but she knew: it was going to happen. Everything was going to happen.

They set out on the climb once more. Twice they met up with the others and then they fell behind again. She had to stop to catch her breath.

"Three more lookouts," Russell told her. "And you'd better hold on to me when you lean over."

"I'm OK. I don't need to hold on."

"We're right near the top now. Three-quarters of an hour and we should be at the end."

"Thank God," she said.

"Are you coming?"

"I'm pretty tired. I think maybe I'll stay here for a while."

"At this stage you should keep moving. Here, I'll help you."

"No," she yelped.

He smiled. He stepped toward her. They were under the overhang, where no one could see. In front of them the snow came to an end, the whole mountain seemed to tumble away downward and then stop—ending in the air, with nothing else beyond but the tiny villages miles below.

She thought she heard a voice. She said, "There's some-body walking behind us."

"There isn't anybody."

"Yes, there is." She rushed away from him, slid back down the way they had come, and kept going. He called after her, "It's only a little way to the top. Come on, Rhoda."

She skidded sideways around the corner and fell. As she got to her feet, she saw Carter moving up along the path. She opened her arms.

"Did you do it?" he said.

"Of course not."

"What the hell are you doing? You got everything all wrong. You were supposed—"

"Please," she said, "let's go. Let's just go back down, please."

"We can't. We've got to go up."

"He's there," she whispered.

He moved his lips silently, asking, "Where?"

"Around the corner." He'd be standing right there, listen-ing. He wouldn't have gone on without her, and he couldn't have seen Carter, because the view was blocked where they were.

"All right," Carter said. "I'll get him. You stay here."

"No," she wailed. She fell down again and clung to his legs. "No. We'll get a divorce."

"I don't want the divorce," he said. "I want the money." He kicked her hard in the ribs.

She let go, staggered to her feet, and tried to steady herself by grabbing his shoulder. He went backward, his mouth open. He was sliding, falling. He went over the edge. She slithered farther down the path, calling out to him, and landed heavily against a mound of snow.

He was gone. There was nothing. The drop was sheer, the precipice so angled that he would have fallen nearly to the bottom of the mountain. She couldn't believe it. He hadn't made a sound. She kept staring as if he might reappear.

"Perfect," Russell said. He was standing at the bend in the path. He might even have seen it happen. She looked up and saw that he was grinning.

"Beautiful," he said. "So, that's him out of the way."

"He just slipped."

"Now there's only you."

"He kept saying you'd killed your first wife."

"Sure. She made some joke about being insured and I realized it would work. It was a gamble. The big ones always pay off, remember? Let's go. We'll have to report it."

She moved carefully toward the outside of the path, near the edge.

"Watch out," he said. "That's dangerous."

"Why should I wait for you to do it some other way?" She was excited and terrified, nearly prepared to throw herself off into the emptiness behind her. She raised one foot, put it down and lifted the other, as if dancing. She said, "He was always a real bastard to me, but I loved him."

"Don't,"he told her.

"Why not? If I jumped, you'd be in it up to your neck, wouldn't you? Two wives going over the brink the same way—I don't think the insurance companies would like that."

"I'd say he did it."

"They wouldn't believe you, Ross." She took another step backward, intoxicated by fear. She could feel the open space drawing her away as if a tide were racing out behind her, pulling. It reminded her of the repeating dream he'd told her about; his nightmares had become hers to live out. She was slipping. She could go, any minute. She played with the last few feet, the last inches. It was like being in the spotlight, surrounded by deathly brilliance, watched by the whole world.

"Don't step back," he shouted. He started to move toward her.

"I loved him," she said. "And Jesus, was he good in bed— he didn't have to get it out of a book."

He came at her, his arms held in front of him, the hands set, ready to push her over.

She waited until he was almost touching her, then she feinted to the side, just as Mr. Moto had taught her to, and knocked his leg out from under him with a sharp kick.

He flew straight into the air, out across the chasm and down. He howled as he went over. And she scrambled to safety; up the path and around the corner. The rescuers would trample on all the prints, so that was all right, and they'd have to take her word for it that the two men had been quarreling about the death of the first wife, but she was pretty sure people would believe her.

She took a deep breath, threw back her head and screamed, a long trembling call of horror. If they'd been in the avalanche season, she could have brought down the mountainside with it. It made no difference now, at this time of year: let them hear it back in the villages and up in the resort hotels. It was the one thing she was good at.

She was crying; bereaved, pretty, a young mother: this time she was the star. Everyone would respect her grief. They'd all be kind to her. When she told her story, saying that Carter and Russell had been fighting, she'd be standing center stage where the brightness of the sky, the white shine from the ice peaks, would beat upon her like limelight on a heroine; like truth itself; till she outshone the light-reflecting surfaces of nature: candid, diamond-dazzling, pure. She screamed and screamed.

ABOUT THE AUTHOR

Rachel Ingalls grew up in Cambridge, Massachusetts. At the age of seventeen she left high school and spent two years in Germany—one living with a family, the second auditing classes at the universities of Göttingen, Munich, Erlangen, and Cologne. After her return to the United States she entered Radcliffe College, where she majored in English. In 1964 she moved to England, where she has been living ever since.

Her novel *Mrs. Caliban*, published in 1982, was selected by the British Book Marketing Council as one of the twenty great postwar American novels. Simon and Schuster published *I See a Long Journey* in 1986, *The Pearlkillers* in 1987, and *Binstead's Safari* in 1988.